RIFT

The Rift Saga, Book 1

RIFT

Andreas Christensen

RIFT

Copyright © Andreas Christensen 2015
All rights reserved
ISBN: 978-1507752746

Cover design: Yoly Cortez, cormarcovers.com
Editor: Shelley Holloway, hollowayhouse.me

This is a work of fiction. All names, characters, places, and incidents are the product of the author's imagination, or used in a fictitious manner. Any resemblance to actual persons, living or dead, businesses, organizations, events or locales is purely coincidental. This book, or parts thereof, may not be reproduced in any form without permission.

RIFT

Prologue

SUE

She moved quietly through the streets. It was after dark, and she wasn't supposed to be out this late. Her mother would be furious, anger fueled with fear. Susan Atlas knew all too well what happened if you were caught outside at this hour. She had almost been caught once before, about a year ago, and though she escaped to safety, her friend Laurie hadn't been so lucky. When he returned after that night in prison, he'd been quiet for days. In general, they all avoided being outdoors at this time of night, unless it was absolutely necessary.

But tonight was the night before Initiation, and everyone from school was gathering outside the gymnasium for a final night together. Tomorrow, some of them would be chosen for Service, many risking their lives while gaining the opportunity for a better life for themselves and their families. Others would not be chosen, and would remain in Charlestown, doomed to a short life of limits and boundaries.

Her father had turned fifty last year.

She missed him tremendously.

Though they were all taught that the Covenant depended on its rules, and that only the Covenant protected them from the world outside, it didn't make it any easier to accept that her father wouldn't be there tomorrow. Ever since she could remember, she had been told that the system could only be sustainable by imposing an upper age limit of fifty on non-citizens, but she didn't know why. And her father had been healthy, a merchant, and a productive member of society. But, as soon as he had turned fifty, he was gone.

She wanted a different life.

She wanted to serve.

A noise from a side street caught her attention. Shuffling feet, sobs, heavy grunts. She stepped closer to the street entrance. In the faint light, she saw three officers and something between them. A man, struggling to remain on his feet. One of the officers shoved his knee into the man's groin, and he doubled over. This couldn't just be someone breaking the curfew.

The man lifted his head, and when the light lit up his swollen face and shaven head, she saw the electronic tattoo across his scalp. Corpus.

What was one of the Corpus doing here, she wondered. But she knew the answer right away. A fugitive.

The Corpus lands lie just south of here, but the boundary—the Belt—was so tight, she had never heard of someone actually escaping. She could understand why someone would try. Within the Corpus, you served until you died, or for a lucky few, until your seven years were up. There was no way out of Service, and with the Corpus, the only way for most was death.

His face had a resigned look, as if he didn't care what happened to him anymore. Even with blood running from his nose and broken teeth, and a deep gash on his temple, a wan smile crossed his bloody lips. She realized she was looking at a man who saw death as a way out. A man free at last. She shuddered and withdrew, afraid that the officers would notice her. But none of them moved away from the fugitive.

Instead, one of them drew his nightstick and adjusted the voltage. She had seen how they did that, depending on how much pain or damage they wanted to inflict-enough to subdue, or enough to incapacitate. She had heard the voltage could be set to kill, though.

"You sure about this, Gunnar?" she heard one of the officers ask. The one with the nightstick grinned, teeth showing in the streetlight.

"This one's done for. He'd be useless, anyway. Let's just get this done, and file the damn report." When no one protested, he set the nightstick against the fugitive's neck.

"Move away, Trace, this will hurt," he said. He pressed something, and the fugitive began to shake violently.

After a moment, the officer withdrew the stick, and the body slumped to the ground. The one called Gunnar kicked the dead man lightly to make sure.

"All right, let's get this one out of here," he said.

Sue withdrew further, shocked at what she had seen. This man had toiled in the Corpus lands, and whatever the officers did to him before they killed him, his expression had told her everything she needed to know.

Tomorrow was Initiation Day, and she might face the same fate that this man had run away from. A chill ran down her spine as she realized this was the last night of the life she had lived until now, and that whatever tomorrow would bring, nothing would ever be the same again.

Chapter 1

SUE

Initiation Day. The day she had always known would come was here at last. In less than two hours, she would be standing in the town square, among the young men and women of Charlestown, many of whom she had known since childhood. Waiting, wondering if they would be chosen. Sue stared at the picture of her family on the wall. Father was gone, and soon she might be gone, too, leaving her mother and Jason alone. It would be hard on them both, but the thought of Jason, eight soon to be nine, who might never see his big sister again, was just too damn hard to think about. Her mother was strong, though, and she would be strong for Jason, just as she had been strong for all three of them when her father had turned fifty. She felt almost relieved that he wouldn't be there to experience the heartbreaking ceremony. She'd seen it on the live screens year after year—a mother breaking down after seeing her child chosen for one of the deadlier services; a father's futile fight to protect his children; sons and daughters being dragged off to serve; siblings seeing their big sister or brother for the last time. It would have broken her father's heart if he were here to see her go. Now, it will be up to her mother to carry on.

Service to the State. A concept pounded into them all ever since they were old enough to understand. The Moon people had taught them that, above all, Service to the State was the greatest virtue. Indeed, it was the single most important duty, which ensured unity, security, and prosperity.

Sue looked away from the family picture and into the mirror. Sometimes, she thought she looked hard—cold and emotionless. It wasn't something she wanted, but life for an English girl in the Covenant would do that to you. Still, she had made herself look her best for today. Her dark hair, almost black, was neatly braided, and she had put on her finest gown, the grey one she only wore at weddings and funerals. Her hazel eyes looked back at her, steady, no more fear. A half-smile crept forth. She was ready. She exhaled slowly, having long ago accepted her fate. If she died in the Service, she would honor her town and her family. And if she survived, she would have a real chance at being chosen for citizenship. And she would change the lives of her mother and little brother.

It didn't mean so much to her personally. After all, she knew very few citizens, and they were no different from the others. Except that they didn't live here, most of them. Most citizens were rich and chose to live off somewhere else, although a few returned to their old hometown. She had heard stories of how some just partied and gorged themselves on food and drink and whatnot, but she knew there were others who used their wealth to help those less fortunate. She hoped to one day be that kind of citizen. She knew what even just one citizen who chose to help could accomplish.

She knew that citizenship was something to be sought after, and a great honor, not just for the one receiving it, but also for the entire community. She recalled what she had learned of citizenship in school. In the beginning, only the Moon people and their descendants were eligible, but within decades, a few of the English were given the opportunity to earn their citizenship through Service. Custom soon became law, and these days, every young man and woman is added to the list the year they turn eighteen. One in twenty is chosen, sometimes fewer. The rest are left to live out their lives in their hometowns, usually a life of poverty. Not being chosen also means a short life, since only citizens are allowed to live past fifty. The euthanasia laws set the life limit to fifty for non-citizens, meaning the English, and forty or thirty-five for the disabled, depending on their disability. But citizens are allowed to live for as long as they choose. And with Moon-people technology, that could be a very long time.

She had no way of knowing which Service she would be picked for, but she was fit, healthy, and had done well in school, so she was pretty sure one of the better Services would select her. A couple of weeks ago, she had even registered her preferences with the Service Bureau. She only did it to make sure they noticed her; she didn't expect the preferences to count for much else. You could often tell, though, to a certain degree, where they would put someone. If you were really smart or had some special talent, you might end up a Student. The strong, agile kind, or the fighters, usually ended up as Janissaries. Sometimes the Wardens would pick one of those, as well, although it was difficult to know what the Wardens were really looking for. The Corpus were the last to pick, and as a result, always got those not chosen for any of the other Services. In the Corpus, the whip ruled, backs were bent, and the will broken. It was the one Service Sue truly dreaded and didn't think she would stand a chance of surviving. Better to be a Janissary. Few made it all the way through Janissary Service, but those who did, always became citizens. Also, it was the only Service that required only three years, instead of the usual seven.

She looked at her watch. Time to go. She had already said her goodbyes, and as was customary, the family never walked with a candidate to the selection ceremony. She might see them there, but if she was chosen, there would be no farewells, no hugs or kisses. That would be seen as disloyal. After all, Service was an honor.

Sue made sure to switch off the light as she left the room. She had a final look around before exiting through the front door. From behind her, she could hear the sobs of little Jason, and her mother comforting him, the soothing words incomprehensible. She knew she would see them again, even if she was chosen. That was what she would live for. That was what she would do whatever it took for.

~

Outside, the noises that usually greeted her had subsided. Today was a public holiday, and only the most necessary functions were still running. Sue heard the train come to a halt a few blocks down to the right and an angry couple shouting at each other in a building nearby. Other than that, there was only the wind and the rustling of leaves. Sue didn't look back as she walked away from the house, passing between the artificial trees on the sidewalk and crossing the street. The grocery store on the other side had a CLOSED sign on the door. She noticed someone moving inside, and smiled. There was always some business to be done, even on Initiation Day; it just happened in behind closed doors.

She passed the butcher shop, the bakery, and the telephone office, without seeing any signs of life. The telephone service was closed, anyway, and even if it wasn't, the lines were all monitored. She remembered two years ago, when Charlestown got its second telephone office on the other side of town. No one could believe there was a need for more than one, but amazingly, both were still in business. There was always someone with family in the next town or business too far away to go speak face to face. You would think people had better things to spend their hard-earned coins on than telephoning each other, but obviously they didn't.

The town square wasn't far, just a few blocks away, and then a wide circle back around, which took her right back toward the train station, located on the far side of the square. This was where everyone was gathered. She glanced up at the three-story building that housed the mayor's office and saw the Covenant flag flapping in the wind, hanging out above the sidewalk. Mayor Robertson was one of the few citizens she knew, and a woman she looked up to. She had earned her citizenship through Service with the Janissaries, and although there were all kinds of stories about her, Sue didn't know which ones to believe. All she knew was that she was a fair but stern woman in her sixties, with a granddaughter a year younger than Sue, and she was from here. She was one of them. That counted for something.

The crowd let her through; some smiled and patted her on the back while others remained silent, wearing solemn looks and somber eyes. Everyone knew that many of the kids they saw today would never return, one way or the other. Sue walked toward the officers, who were directing everyone into lines where they would wait to be registered. She noticed a couple from school being separated. Who knew if they would ever see each other again? A mother kissed a boy from her class on the forehead, tears running down her cheeks, before the officers separated them. While the son was taken away, the mother didn't make a sound. Her lips moved constantly, though, a silent prayer for her son to return. She saw Chas from the advanced class, nodding at his father, both of them wearing determined looks in their eyes.

She joined Vince and Laurie at the back of the line, as the officer directing her turned and went to fetch another. Both were laughing, although she sensed their nervousness. Laurie's sister had been chosen by the Janissaries last year, and he hoped to join her up north if he was chosen today. Vince on the other hand, had no desire to join his older brother. He'd been chosen for the Corpus three years ago, and no one had heard from him since. They would have heard if he was dead, but if he wasn't, he would be soon enough, once they had spent him. Sue remembered Vince saying once that it was better to think that he died that fateful day. Better to mourn and move on.

"You nervous?" Laurie asked. Sue just nodded.

"Come on, man, we're all nervous here," Vince said. "All we can do now is hope. It's all decided for us, anyways."

"You really believe that, Vince?" Sue asked, cocking

her head. Vince had been talking to the priest lately, and their belief was that everything was decided by fate. There was no escaping it, and whatever you did to avoid your fate, eventually it caught up to you. Better to accept it, embrace it, and gather strength from it.

"Yeah, I do. I really do. I just hope fate has something better in store for me than my bro." Sue watched him. A year ago, Vince had started working out, training, in order to be more attractive to the Janissaries. It was the best he could hope for, as the Students were out of the question. Anything but the Corpus. A few months ago, though, Vince had started slacking off, as the faith had started to sink in. There was nothing he could do; the Corpus were just as likely as the Janissaries to pick a healthy, fit young man for Service. And whatever he did, fate would find him eventually.

Sue didn't know what to believe. She listened to the priests, and there was wisdom in their words, but she didn't like the fact that she didn't have a say in it. She had a hard time accepting that her life and death were at the hands of some unknown entity, and that her actions didn't mean anything.

When they reached the front of the line, an officer scanned and registered their IDs and their retinas, and they were allowed to pass.

"Hurry up and wait," Laurie said dryly. Sue looked

back and watched the lines still snail forward. It would be a while until everyone was registered. She looked around to see if her mother and Jason had come. She didn't see them anywhere, but she was certain they were there, somewhere. She noticed her neighbor Marie standing just behind the officers, over by the fence, and saw she was looking at her. Sue smiled.

"Don't bother," Vince said. "You are a candidate now. Property of the State." Sue looked around and noticed that they were all surrounded by officers, keeping them away from the spectators. Then she looked back to Marie, her mother's friend. Did she come here today for her? She would never know.

DAVE

Dave shouldn't be afraid. After all, there was only one option as far as he was concerned; one that would give him the chance to achieve his lifelong dream. He knew he wasn't Janissary material, and the Corpus? No, there were too many other able bodies that would last longer in the Service than he would, with his skinny legs and awkward hands. His mind was his foremost asset, and today, it would give him the future so few could even hope for. Dave was top of his class on the Overall Scholarly Aptitude Test and had received merits for Physics. If anyone in this town was ever a natural Student it would be he. The principal had even congratulated him on his last day at school, asking him not to forget about his hometown when he left to make a name for himself.

So why did he feel this nagging chill down his spine as he passed the officers in front of the town square? Was it fear of rejection? The thought that even he wasn't good enough to be chosen? He looked around and saw familiar faces everywhere. Charlestown was a small community of a few thousand, close to the Belt, separating them from the forbidden areas of the Corpus to the south. It was nothing like the crowded cities to the north, where thousands upon thousands were stacked on top of each other in tall skyscrapers, where you could live your entire life and never know your closest neighbors.

Dave had always liked it here, in this quiet corner of the Covenant. Yes they were poor, but they cared for each other. If someone didn't have enough to eat, or shelter over their heads, people would help out in whatever way they could. If you stumbled, a friend would help you back on your feet. And there had been no uprisings here since the great one, and that was generations ago. Even then, Charlestown had stayed mostly out of the fighting.

Still, he knew he wouldn't have much of a future here, and although his dreams were different from many of his friends who had trained for years to be considered by the Janissaries, his dreams were no less dependent on the outcome of this day.

He glimpsed Sue and Vince and Laurie standing in line for registration, and wondered if he'd ever see them again after today. They had grown up in the same part of town and spent their childhood years making all kinds of mischief together. He'd been placed in an advanced class three years ago, so they didn't meet as often as they used to, but he still considered them his friends.

An officer directed him to the back of a shorter line, and his mind drifted off, while the line slowly snaked forward. When he reached the officer in the front, he started. He hadn't noticed. He fumbled as he produced his ID, and the officer scanned it. Then his retinas were scanned, and he was ushered past, to more waiting. He saw Chas and Felicia from class standing close by, so he went to join them.

"Hey, Dave," Felicia said, while Chas just nodded to him.

"Hey, guys." There wasn't much else to say. Everyone knew what happened next; they'd all seen it several times before. And now it was their turn. Dave didn't really suspect any surprises. The three of them were the smartest in class, according to the tests. They would likely all be chosen for the Students, although Dave noticed an edge to Felicia's voice.

Normally, three to five Student Initiates were chosen from Charlestown, but the number varied, and no one could be absolutely certain. And of the three, Felicia was the weakest.

"Let's get on with it already," Chas said, jaws clenched. It was no secret that Chas thought this ceremony to be a ridiculous artifact, devoid of any real function. Even though officially, the representatives of the Services would make their final decisions right here, today, everyone knew the lists were prepared in advance. If not, there would have been instances of different Services choosing the same Initiates, and it never happened.

The square was filling up, and finally all the lines were empty. The officers formed a half circle behind them. As of this moment, they were all candidates, to be picked for any of the Services, regardless of personal preference. As soon as their names were spoken, their status would change to Initiate. Initiates were taken away immediately and would not be back for as long as their Service lasted, if ever. The remaining candidates would be asked to volunteer. Normally, the only Service that would take volunteers was the Corpus, always in need of more bodies to exploit for the good of the State. Whoever volunteered for the Corpus would have to be desperate—starving or on the run from something. The Janissaries might also take volunteers, if the losses on the front were exceptionally high. The North was constantly at war, but even if they accepted volunteers, the Janissaries were picky. The Students never took volunteers, though; the few Initiates they did take were chosen long before today.

Screens flickered, and a familiar face beamed before them. Head Servant Alexej Lunde, pure Moon blood all the way back to the Descent, and a few steps behind, his mysterious advisor Mark Novak.

"Welcome, candidates," Head Servant Lunde said in a rumbling voice.

"On this day of Initiation, the greatest honor of the Covenant, and the greatest sacrifice, is about to be bestowed upon a select few of the young men and women of Charlestown. Today, those with the skills and abilities needed to become our future citizens will be chosen for the highest glory of all, known as Service to the State."

Chapter 2

SUE

The huge screens made everything appear closer, and the greatest of them all sat in the front, above the podium. Sue could almost feel the eyes of Head Servant Lunde staring straight at her. Of course, it wasn't real. Head Lunde and Counselor Novak were hundreds of miles away, in Legacy, the great sprawling capital, where most citizens lived, and the only place in which Moon people made up the majority. As far as she knew, no head servant had ever set foot in Charlestown.

"I welcome you all here today, to the annual selection of candidates. To remember how our great nation once rose from the ashes, like the phoenix of ancient mythology, a feat accomplished only because of the sacrifices and service to the common good made by our predecessors.

Long ago, these acts became an example of how one person's Service can benefit all, for generations to come, and therefore, Service to the State became one of the founding pillars of our society. Only those who are willing and able to serve are worthy of citizenship. And capable of carrying the burden of responsibility that citizenship carries with it. And so, with no further ado, I welcome the representatives of the Services." Sue looked down to the podium below the screen and saw four figures rise from their chairs, while Mayor Robertson remained seated.

The first to step forward was Dr. Erle Nielsen, the senior scholar, an ageless woman with long grey wisps of hair, small glasses that threatened to fall off the tip of her nose, and a smile that never seemed to break through her absentminded demeanor.

"I'll make this quick," she said, producing a crumpled piece of paper.

"I welcome Initiates Chas Drummond and Felicia Petit to the Students." She paused for a moment, scanning the crowd. "Yes, that was it." She finished, crumpled the paper back up, and put it in her pocket. Sue frowned. She would have thought Dave to be a natural Student, but she knew they were extremely selective. Two Students from Charlestown this year then. Well, she'd seen worse.

"First Janissary Ivanov," a booming voice announced, and an imposing figure, six feet tall, athletic, with short white hair, and clad in the customary black, took a step forward. A perfect face marred only by a long scar running from his temple to his jaw, set in stone.

"To the Janissaries, I welcome Initiates Susan Atlas, Frederick Burke Lowe, Hugh Winters, John Victor Preston,

The Students wore white, while the Warden Initiates put on green. The Corpus took a while to gather, but once they were all there, they were given red armbands, while officers paid close attention. It wasn't unheard of that fresh Initiates tried to run, and those chosen by the Corpus had less to lose than the others.

Dr. Nielsen just waved an officer over to gather her Initiates, and Chas and Felicia looked more than ready to get moving. The Whip Master didn't even look at the Initiates wearing their red armbands. Some were sobbing, while others seemed to let all hope die, steeling themselves for whatever might come next. First Janissary Ivanov walked around, looking each of his Initiates up and down, speaking a few words with each and every one. When he stopped in front of Dave, he seemed to wrinkle his nose at his skinny bones.

"Initiate Wagner. It seems we've got quite a challenge here. Well, we'll just have to try to make a Janissary out of you, kid. Any questions?" Dave seemed to hesitate before he answered.

"Sir, I wonder if there's been a mistake..." he said, before trailing off.

"Speak up, boy. Here's your chance," the First Janissary barked.

"Sir, I don't think I'm Janissary material. I mean, I'm the highest ranked for academic achievements. In school. I wonder if there's any chance of being transferred to the Students?"

God, how can you be so stupid, Dave? Sue thought. She wanted to scream at him to stop. She almost expected the First Janissary to slap him or something. But Ivanov just nodded and seemed to consider what Dave had said.

"I think you're right, son. You don't look like you have what it takes at all." A smirk crept across the face of the older man, and Sue shivered.

"Sadly, Dr. Nielsen just left, and I won't be able to reach her for a while. But I think I know someone else who would have use for your talents." He looked over at the Whip Master, and Sue saw sweat break on Dave's forehead, as he struggled to say something. He remained silent, though his face turned pale and his eyes closed as the First Janissary moved on.

As he reached Sue, she felt herself shrink before his eyes.

"Initiate Atlas. I fear we are out of time, as the train leaves in fifteen minutes." Sue was torn between self-preservation and friendship, but in the end, friendship won. She spoke just as Ivanov moved to turn away.

"Sir. I think it would be a waste to send Initiate Wagner to the Corpus. Look at him. He'd be dead meat in a month. What kind of Service would that be, sir? Perhaps the

Wardens would take him?" She had no idea what the Wardens actually did, as most of it was secret, and there were few, if any, Wardens from Charlestown. But the way she saw it, anything would be better that the Corpus. The First Janissary fumed and was about to lash out at her, probably ready to trade her black armband for a red one, when the Master Warden interjected.

"She's right, Ivanov. It would be a waste." He smiled.

"We'll take him." The First Janissary looked furiously from Sue to the Master Warden, and then back again at Sue. Then he exhaled and shook his head.

"All right then, enough of this nonsense." He turned toward the Master Warden. "Take the boy. Now, let's get on with this. Damn kids need to learn some respect." The last was murmured as he walked off, signaling the officers to take the Janissary Initiates to the waiting train. As the Corpus Initiates walked off to the southbound train, the others followed their representatives toward the trains that would take them north. Dave followed the Master with the three other Warden Initiates, and as he passed Sue, his lips moved, mouthing a silent thank you. Sue smiled briefly, although she was angry with him for opening his mouth. *That head of his will get him in trouble again*, she thought. And the next time, she wouldn't be there to save him.

Sue wondered if she had just made a huge mistake.

She wasn't the most social, but as far as she knew, she'd never had an enemy. As she boarded the train, she caught the eye of the First Janissary and wondered if she'd made her first.

~

Sue found a vacant seat by the window and sat down. After a minute or so, Laurie came and sat down next to her.

"So, you know how far north we're going?" he asked. Sue shook her head.

"No idea. Never been north of Stonehaven," she said. Stonehaven lay inland, northwest of Charlestown, and was the town everyone went to for trade goods that were hard to come by at home. She had gone there with her father once, while her mother and little Jason stayed at home. Thinking of her little brother almost choked her up, and she turned and stared out the window. They were going faster than she'd expected. The train hovered inches above the tracks, and the smoothness of the ride was amazing. Not like riding the steam cars back home. She'd done that once, too.

"It's magnetic. Maglev, I think it's called," Laurie said. She turned back and looked at him. Curly, dark hair, wide lips and nose, and originally the prankster among them, he'd changed after his sister was chosen. *More serious*, Sue thought.

"We have no idea what to expect, do we?" she said. He half-smiled back.

"Guess we don't." He leaned forward to see better. "We haven't heard from Lisa since last Initiation Day. Not one word."

They both stared out for what seemed forever, and Sue felt herself doze off as daylight receded. The train suddenly slowed, and they emerged from a tunnel. In the distance, they could see the capital, Legacy, in its entire splendor. Lights everywhere; no shortage of electricity there. And soon, the train stopped on the platform. This was clearly separate from the civilian platforms, as there were officers everywhere, herding groups of Initiates around. Black, white, and green armbands still separated the Initiates, while the officers wore the grey uniforms she was familiar with from back home.

Their train car was Janissaries only, but she knew Dave, Chas, Felicia, and the others from Charlestown were on the same train. Now though, their ways parted. She saw a group with green armbands boarding another train; no familiar faces, though.

"There go the Wardens," Laurie said quietly. The Wardens were something of a secret society, especially since there were so few from Charlestown. The rumors said the Wardens mostly stayed in the West, even further than the miner towns and wildlife preserves. But no one knew for sure. Initiates from Charlestown generally went to the

Janissaries or the Corpus, with a few now and then to the Students. Student Initiates rarely returned to their hometowns. After having served their seven years and earning their citizenship, many chose to stay on in the Service to become Scholars.

While the Students were treated well enough to not only survive their seven years, but thrive, the Corpus spent their Initiates and spewed out what was left. Usually that wasn't much; if they even made it through, they returned home with disabled bodies and broken minds, though their citizen pensions could easily feed a family for the rest of their lives. The Janissaries had a high casualty rate, but those who survived were awarded citizenship and if they chose to return to their hometowns, they did so with fanfare—the pride of the town. Every time one did, it was cause for celebration.

So, since the Corpus was an absolute horror, the Wardens were a mystery, and the few that were chosen for the Students were always from the advanced class, whenever Sue and her friends had discussed the prospect of Service, they had implicitly discussed service with the Janissaries.

Sue saw Chas and Felicia pass right outside their window and waved at them. Felicia noticed and waved back, while Chas seemed to be lost in thought. They would be taken to the Legacy Academy or the Covenant University, which both produced scholars. Sue didn't really know the difference between the two, and right now, she didn't care. She just hoped her friends would fare well.

"I was worried for Vince there for a second," Laurie said. Sue smiled.

"We all were. I was so certain he'd be chosen. He'll be fine back home." she said.

"Yeah, better than the Corpus," Laurie said, as he sat back, ignoring the window and staring up at the ceiling. The train started moving again. Slowly at first, but soon it was moving at top speed again.

"Still going north," Sue murmured, as sleep seemed to pull at her again.

She was almost out when the doors to their train car slid open and a man clad in Janissary black entered.

"Listen up," he said, loud enough to wake those who'd dozed off. Laurie sat up straighter, and Sue craned to see better. The man was lean and tall, and when Sue looked closer, she saw he couldn't be more than twenty-five or so; it was the trimmed beard that made him look older.

"In an hour, you will enter Camp Sharpe, where you will begin your training. In the meantime, you are to read this information sheet." He produced a stack of papers, and started passing them out.

"You can all read—the Janissaries have no need for illiterates—so I suggest you pay attention to everything this sheet tells you. On arrival, we expect you to know this by heart." He let the Initiates pass the sheets along, and turned back. Just before the sliding door, he turned again.

"Initiates, in one hour, the toughest part of your lives will begin. For some, it will be the final part. No matter how well prepared you think you are, make no mistake; the coming days and weeks will test you. Everyone has a limit, and we intend to find yours. One day, you might find these trials will save the lives of yourself and those around you." Sue found herself absorbing the advice, and although his words were disturbing, they also made her eager. She had felt that way ever since hearing her name being called by First Janissary Ivanov, and as the train took them north, the feeling had grown stronger. The Janissary hadn't finished though.

"One more piece of advice for you. I know many of you are friends. You've gone to school together, grown up together, played together, in Holstonhead, Morrow, Fort Winter, Stonehaven, Charlestown, or wherever.

I want you to forget all that. Forget your hometown and everyone there. Forget your best friend from kindergarten. Forget your boyfriend or girlfriend or whatever. It's all history, and you are about to be reborn as Janissaries. And let me tell you, a Janissary is sworn to Service. To the *State*. Not to your pals or your birth family or your town. The State.

"You may at some point find yourselves torn between loyalties, in training or in actual combat. It may be hard to abandon someone you played with as a child, or the person you first kissed, leaving him or her to die in some godforsaken ditch up north. Or to carry out punishment on someone you knew back when you were kids for having disobeyed the tranquility laws. But that's what it takes to fulfill your obligations—to serve. And I want you to remember this: Many of you will die in the Service. Almost everyone you knew in that place you've always called home will die within just a few decades. In fifty years, even that cute little baby next door or little cousin Vinny will be dead. But, if you survive your three years of Service, you may live on for a century, if not more. Should you earn your citizenship, any children you have will automatically be citizens. In addition, you may choose one family member to be given the status of probationary citizen. One. The rest of your family will be well off, but they will still only be able to live until the age of fifty.

"But fifty years from now, when your hometown doesn't feel like home anymore, you will have new friends. You will have a new family—people who are not subject to the euthanasia laws, who understand what you've been through. You will be part of the Covenant, having earned your privileges and your status." He stood quiet for a moment before leaving through the sliding doors, letting the

Initiates absorb what he had told them. Sue and Laurie looked at each other, and Sue felt an urge to protest. But she didn't.

Instead, she looked at the sheet of paper and started to read. It was all basic instructions: how to salute a superior, a chart for arranging her clothes and personal items in her locker, fire instructions, the different alerts that might occur, and some basic information on what to expect in their first few days at Camp Sharpe.

She didn't speak to Laurie for the rest of the ride, and she wondered if it was because they were both busy studying the information sheet, or if it was because of what the Janissary had said. She knew Laurie would always be her friend, and wanted to dismiss what the man had said, but somewhere in the back of her mind, she wondered if there wasn't a lot of truth to it, as well. After all, many of the Initiates right here in this train car *would* die, and soon. And there was no doubt that the euthanasia laws were merciless. On your fiftieth birthday, you were given the choice of how to go. Most took the pill, and that was that. In a few years, her neighbor, who had shown up for Initiation Day in the town square, would be gone. The baker across the street had taken the pill last year, and next year, it was his wife's turn.

Sue felt the train decelerate, and as it slowed to a crawl, they entered a tunnel. Seconds turned to minutes, and after what felt like an eternity, the train exited the tunnel and stopped on a platform bathed in light. It was late evening outside, and darkness had descended. Behind the platform stood two black towers with moving flood lights, and as the lights moved around, she saw parts of Camp Sharpe, where she would spend the next several weeks in training. On the platform stood Janissaries, a row of them a few paces apart. From what she had read on the info sheet, these were senior Janissaries, who would each take a small group to their quarters and get them all settled in, let them know how things worked and how to behave, so when basic training began, they would be as ready as they could be. After sticking her head out for Dave, she thought it would be best to be as anonymous as possible and not draw attention to her. She looked up at the Covenant flag flapping in the wind on top of the main house in front of the platform. The white circle with another white round dot just above and to the right, on a black background speckled with small, paler dots. The Earth, the Moon, and the stars. The Moon people had saved them all, and the flag signified how Earth had been reborn in the image of their saviors. Now, it was her turn to serve, to carry on the responsibilities of protecting the Covenant.

DAVE

The train moved quietly through the rolling hills, and the only sound was the low chatter among initiates. The further west they went, the more sparse the habitation. Finally, there was nothing but untouched nature as far as the eye could see. Dave knew he should get some sleep, but he was far too nervous to even try. There weren't many Warden initiates, and most were from places he'd barely heard of. He didn't know the others from Charlestown well, and even they mostly kept to themselves. He had no idea what to expect.

One thing he knew was that the Wardens were a mystery in themselves. Another was that no one told him anything, even though he noticed some of the initiates talked to each other as if they knew more than he did. He just sat there by himself, staring out the window as the train sped west through the rolling hills and the valley beyond, which he'd only read about in school textbooks. Soon, he was farther west than he'd ever been, further than anyone was allowed. Obviously, the Wardens were allowed out here, though.

So when the train slowed down and finally came to a stop, he was dead tired and excited all at once. A man in olive fatigues and a shaggy beard ushered them out of the train car and onto a platform where several others were waiting. Most wore the same fatigues, but he noticed that, although they had some resemblance to the militaristic Janissaries, with uniforms and certainly a chain of command of sorts, these looked like they all had adapted their individual styles. There were those with bandanas and hats, but also uncovered heads, shades, electronic tattoos—but very different from the Corpus tattoos, and even a few short sleeves. Off in a corner of the platform, a couple of young men and a woman were smoking, a sickly sweet scent that told him this was definitely an illegal substance. He'd never actually smelled it, let alone smoked it, but he remembered learning about it once, in class. They said it was dangerous and would kill you. When they noticed him staring, they grinned at him and laughed, and he quickly averted his eyes.

"Hey! Watch where you're going," one of the other initiates, a girl, said. She smiled as he fumbled and almost lost his footing. She was lean and looked fit, with full lips and auburn, close-cropped hair. He'd noticed her boarding the train at one of the last stops, and she was one of those initiates who already seemed to know her way around. She offered her hand.

"Liz." He took her hand and shook it.

"Dave."

"I guess you haven't tried kissweed before, have you?" she said. He shook his head. She chuckled, but didn't say anything. A grey-bearded fellow who stood out, not just because of his multi-colored shirt, but also because he was obviously an authority here, walked across the platform and stood in front of them.

"All right, Initiates, listen up," he said loud enough for everyone to hear.

"I'll make no speeches, I promise. I just want you to know that you are welcome, and that I hope you will settle in here. In the next few weeks, you will learn more of the Wardens, and our role in the Covenant." He paused, a knowing smile breaking through the thick beard.

"Trust me; you don't know half of it." And with that, he turned and left, leaving the initiates standing idly.

"Well, that was brief," Liz said. Dave wondered what would happen next, and he didn't have to wait for long. A lanky fellow, around twenty-five, with sand-colored hair and sunburned skin, with those strange-looking tattoos snaking up his neck, came up to them, carrying an infopad. He wore a nametag that said "Searles."

"Names," he said, sounding almost bored. They gave him their names, and he found them on his list.

"Wagner, you're in B-house. It's the first one on the left. Sidnell, follow that chubby fellow, and he'll take you to your house. You're in A," he said. They both nodded, and Searles walked over to another group of initiates.

"I guess we'll see each other around then," Liz said.

"Sure. Nice to meet you."

Dave watched her walk away, and turned to see who else was there. One of the initiates from Charlestown, Brian something, was lingering, and Dave walked over to him. They nodded at each other, and Dave thought he remembered where he'd seen him before.

"Did you compete in the math fair last year?" he asked. Brian nodded and grinned.

"Yeah. No idea why I even made it to the finals; never been any good at it before or since, but my teacher thought I had a head for it. No match for you though." Dave remembered. He'd ended up second, beaten only by Chas. Brian, from a different school, had been pretty good, but nothing like Chas or himself. Smart, but poorly educated.

"So, what do you think all this is? I mean, no one ever told us what the Wardens actually do," Brian said. Dave just shrugged.

"No idea. But it must have something to do with our location. We are pretty far west, probably deep into forbidden territory. And from what I can tell, most initiates seem smart. Not Student smart, perhaps, but intelligence seems to be a criteria. And independence perhaps? They don't look very disciplined," he said, gesturing at the kissweed smokers. Brian nodded.

"I guess we'll know soon enough. It's just that I hate being kept in the dark." Dave smiled.

"Maybe that's another criterion? Curiosity?"

It turned out Brian was also to be living in B-house, so they walked together. It was nice to have a familiar face around, with everything else new and unknown. Dave realized he'd made two new friends in just a short while. Usually, he wasn't the type to make friends easily, so this was something new for him. He figured he might fit in just fine here.

Chapter 3

SUE

"Move, you lazy bastards!" the tacticus yelled. Sue gritted her teeth and kept running, despite the metallic taste of blood in her mouth, her lungs screaming for air and her muscles begging for just a brief respite. She kept moving, because whatever she did, she would not be among the washouts. After just three weeks, many had already gone south, kicked out for failing to meet the rigorous standards of the Janissaries.

Basic training was by far the toughest challenge she'd ever faced, except for dealing with the death of her father, of course. The tacticus in charge of her team of initiates was an imposing figure, a suntanned face with blue eyes and hard angular features, hair and mustache the color of sand. His name was Hordvik. She had begun to notice most of the officers were Moon people, and although tacticus wasn't strictly an officer rank, she hadn't seen too many English ranking above senior Janissary. Hordvik behaved as if used to command, even though he couldn't be more than a few years older than she was. And indeed, those of Moon blood she had encountered so far all seemed bred to command, bred for war. She wondered if there were any English at all ranked above tacticus. It was difficult to think that way, without wondering how many of the initiates would last through basic, but as soon as the thought hit her, she forced it away. No use thinking about it. If it happened, it happened.

"What the hell are you doing, Atlas? Move it!" she heard Tac Hordvik yelling. She picked up her pace, just to avoid being singled out. The punishment for not giving your everything was harsh enough, but finding yourself the mark of a bullying tacticus could break you. *No more thinking now*, she thought. *Just keep moving.*

She was all spent when Tac Hordvik ordered them to halt. She had to exert herself just to keep standing, but through the fog of exhaustion, she saw another officer walking up to the tacticus.

"Sir, Team One Three Charlie ready, sir!" Hordvik said, standing at attention. She saw the two silver stars of the other officer. Sub meridian, she rehearsed quietly. She still didn't have the ranks all sorted out. She did know a sub meridian outranked the tacticus, though. She tried reciting the ranks. The initiates were the lowest of the low, at the bottom of the ladder, barely worth their boots. Then came the junior Janissaries. Nobody used the junior prefix, though, except a senior, if he meant to put down the former. Junior Janissaries were those who had passed basic, weapons, and tactical training. Once you gained the single JJ bar, you were deemed combat ready, if only for gunner duty. Meaning cannon fodder. For more skilled tasks, there were senior Janissaries, who had at least three months of JJ duty behind them. Next came the sub tacticus and the tacticus, team ranks still, but the only commanding ranks open to the English, it seemed.

"I see you are driving them hard, Tac Hordvik," the sub meridian stated. The tacticus puffed out his chest.

"I do my best, sir," he answered. The officer clearly liked the response, short and without any fluff, as he nodded.

"Well, Tac, I see that. Keep doing what you're doing, and you might actually make Janissaries out of this lot after all," he said. Sue thought the two looked alike, but it was the same with so many of the Moon people. They even had similar names.

They were given a short break, to hydrate and check for blisters on their feet. Five minutes later, they were up and running again, and Sue wondered if the break had actually made them more tired. She certainly felt that way. She began rehearsing the ranks system again.

The teams were the smallest unit in the Janissaries, except for patrols, which were units put together for a specific mission, and didn't have permanent members. Each team was usually headed by either a tacticus or a head tacticus, which was the lowest official officer rank. Three or four teams made up a squadron, which was led by a sub meridian or a meridian. Three or four squadrons made a battalion, usually led by a meridian or sometimes a head meridian. Altogether, the initiates in basic training had made up a battalion when they began, but now, just three weeks into it, she guessed there couldn't be more than two squadrons left, tops.

Once they finished their training, they would be assigned to one of the brigades, which were self-contained fighting units holding their particular sectors along with air or, in the far eastern sectors, sea support. Brigades were commanded by a sub strategos. And then there were the battle groups, which included at least two Janissary brigades, and commanded their own air and sea support. The battle group was commanded by a strategos, the highest rank found in the Janissaries, except for the First Janissary.

She had wondered at first, whether she would be able to try out for Air or Sea Service, but quickly learned that these units were made up of pure Moon people only, and all their training was kept separate from the Janissaries. Air and Sea only submitted to Janissary command when part of a battle group, which meant that even the lowest airman never took orders from Janissaries below the rank of strategos. She found that curious, but after what happened to one of the initiates who asked too many questions, she had learned to keep her mouth shut. Albert she thought his name was, from

Holstonhead. One day, he was gone, washed out, she heard someone say. Another said she heard one of the officers talking about this kid from Holstonhead, who was transferred to the Corpus. From that moment on, she made it a point not to get singled out, and so far so good.

She had found, in the few spare moments between rigorous training sessions meant to harden them physically and mentally, that she was forming bonds with her teammates. None of her friends from Charlestown were on her team. She had seen Laurie once, while she was standing in line for breakfast, and he had seemed sullen and depressed. When she asked him, he told her of his sister, who had died in combat just a few weeks before their arrival. Sue knew he had hoped to connect with her, and she worried that the loss might hurt his morale enough to get him kicked out. There was nothing she could do for him, though, since the teams were generally kept separated. Sue hadn't seen Laurie since, which was almost a week ago. She hoped he'd be able to pull himself together, or else he might end up in the Corpus.

Still, there was Brad from Morrow, Keisha from Fort Winter, just southwest of here, and Julian from Bunkerville. All friends, growing tighter with every trial they faced together.

On the opposite end, there was Quinn, a volunteer from Hodgeton who seemed to find great joy in the fact that

Keisha struggled with keeping up from time to time. Also, she had learned that Julian had difficulty reading, and Quinn seemed to enjoy taunting him for it, telling him how difficult a time he would face, once they moved on to weapons training, and how much they were required to read in order to make it through.

Still, even with the hardships, and despite scumbags such as Quinn, Sue found herself becoming part of something, and she was beginning to think that the Janissaries might, in time, become her family, as well.

~

A mannequin stood before the initiates, empty eyes staring straight through them, arms hanging motionless. The black suit covering it from neck to toes was unlike anything Sue had ever seen. It was a Janissary battle dress. Unlike the formal parade uniform she had seen so many times, which was tight-fitting and made of some shiny fabric, this one seemed bulky. It was matte, and the black looked almost gray because of thousands of tiny sensors covering its entire surface. Beside the mannequin lay a visored helmet, with tubes and wires obviously meant to connect it to the suit when worn.

"Looks impressive, doesn't it?" Tac Hordvik said, grinning. "Not some parade uniform, but the real thing, built for fighting." Sue looked at the tacticus. He was of the Moon people, with distinct, angular features and the bearing of a man whose heritage was something he always measured himself up against.

"Some of you may come to love the battle dress, those of you who get a chance to wear it in combat, for it will save your life." He looked at every one of them, taking his time. There were nine left from her initiate squadron. From her team, all except Albert were still there, meaning that the other teams had taken harder losses. Sue was glad to still have Brad, Julian, and Keisha, but she would have been even happier if she didn't have to deal with Quinn.

"In the Janissaries, you should expect injuries. You may stand too close to a blast, get caught up in a chemical attack, or get sprayed by a hail from a machine gun, storming an enemy position. And the battle dress will be the only thing standing between you and glory. *Meaning death*, Sue thought.

"A Janissary and his suit are as one single organism. It's like a symbiosis, where if you treat your suit well, it will keep you alive. Sensors all over, both on the outside and inside, will notice subtle changes in you and your environment. The powerful AI knows your needs even before you do, and acts accordingly, sending its little nano bots out to fix you up, or giving you whatever you need to survive a tight situation." The tacticus walked slowly from side to side, and Sue listened intently as he explained some of the battle suit's functionality.

"Of course, it protects you from most small-arms fire, blast and fragments. But it can do so much more. Say you're dead tired from days of fighting, or lying surrounded, enemies all around, and yet you struggle to keep awake. If you fall asleep, you may not be able to get out of a sticky situation. And all the while, your eyes keep sliding shut, and you have trouble keeping a clear thought. Well, the suit will notice, and when you reach a certain level of fatigue, the suit will inject stimulants directly into your blood stream. Enough to keep you from falling asleep if you need to lie still, or enough to give you a real adrenaline boost if the situation demands it." Sue looked at the suit again. An AI to make life or death decisions almost frightened her. But she also knew there were situations where you needed to act quickly, and one day, the suit's abilities might save her life.

"Sometimes, though, even Janissaries need to sleep. The suit can fix that, too. Just tell the AI, and it will help you find the rest you need, through chemical and electrical stimuli of certain parts of your brain. Heck, you can even set the timer." Tac Hordvik chuckled, and a few of the initiates smiled, as well. The tacticus stopped and looked at them. His ice blue eyes sometimes unnerved her. Moon people eyes.

"Imagine being alone out there. Near the coast, the fog can get as thick as soup, and your line of sight stretches no more than a few meters in front of you. The suit can warn you of an enemy's approach long before your eyes can see them and pinpoint their exact location. And if you're incapacitated, the suit can disperse a poisonous gas that kills up to fifteen meters away. Of course, you won't be harmed, as you will be injected with an antidote.

"Later, we will have a look at the nano bots, but suffice it to say, those little fellas will become your best friends, keeping your visor clean, your suit tight, and even stitch you up when needed." He looked straight at her, and Sue looked away for a second. When she looked back, his eyes were still on her.

"Lots of people think they know a Janissary. People all over the Covenant have seen the proud Janissaries parading in their black uniforms. This, though, is the true color of our Service. The battle dress is what sets us apart from our enemies. We have powerful weapons, just as they do. They have just as much conviction and determination as we do, just as much of a purpose and faith and fervor. They have amazing fighting skills, and their soldiers are just as well trained as ours. But our suits keep us alive and help us win, even when outnumbered ten to one. Without a functional suit, we're just as vulnerable as they are. But with the suit powered and active, we are close to invincible."

DAVE

Dave was struggling to find a comfortable position, sitting with the other initiates, while a Warden, probably not more than a couple of years older than he was, lectured.

"You all know the story, or at least the parts taught in schools, and I expect you to know the basics already. Yesterday, we covered the Fall, where humanity descended into darkness. The Fall is where the history books all begin, so let's just leave it at that for now. The Dark Age lasted for almost half a century, forty-seven years to be exact. There was no hope in sight, just a scattering of surviving groups, soon only descendants of those who survived the actual impacts, which killed most of humanity," the Warden intoned, clearly bored from having told the same story too many times. Dave was finally finding a good position and tried to pay more attention. He'd never been that interested in history, so occasionally, there were nuggets he'd never heard before.

"Then came the Descent, in which the Moon people brought salvation. Shortly after landing, they began gathering the scattered groups and communities of the land, one by one. In the beginning, the people were simply cared for—sheltered, fed, and protected. Then, as more began to show up, this started to become increasingly difficult. So, just a few years after the Descent, the Moon people made one demand. In order to receive help, a number of people had to make a contribution. For seven years, those selected would serve obediently, in order to feed, shelter, and protect the others. Thus, the first Covenant was born. The first Service was the Corpus, and it was back-breaking work. Cleaning rubble, cleansing contaminated land, clearing fields, road building, sowing and plowing, building, constructing. Hard, manual labor. Many didn't make the seven years, but the Moon people demanded that everyone stayed until their term was up. And through those hard years, the foundation and principles of Corpus that we know today were created. Eventually, the need arose for different kinds of services, and the Janissaries were created. Enemies were trying to capture revived lands, both in the North and the South, and the Janissaries became the most powerful fighting force on the ground. Supported by the Moon people's air and sea power, the Janissaries swept south and subdued all enemies all the way down to the Floral Sea. With the South conquered, it quickly became apparent that there was no way the Moon people could control such large areas of land unless the conquered peoples became part of the growing nation. And so, thirty years after the Descent, the second Covenant was formed, in which the southern peoples committed to the same allegiance to the common good as those who had gone before them. They would be eligible for Service, the first years only in the Corpus and then later in the Janissaries, and in return, the families of those serving would receive enough food and goods to live out the life of the serving family member. Eventually, most of the fertile lands of the south became State property, run by the Corpus, although some parts became ordinary towns and villages, as well, such as Charlestown and Stonehaven." The Warden paused, and Dave thought of how he'd never realized there had been more than one Covenant. The pact that bound them all together must have been revised several times over. In school, he'd always thought the Covenant to be something that had always been there. Now, as he listened intently, despite the lecturer's obvious boredom, he found that he was learning something new with every sentence.

"So now there was peace in the South, and the second Covenant lasted for seventy-two years. In the North, the wars continued, lasting for months and years at a time, but there were no clear winners. The northern enemies never managed to capture land for more than brief periods, while the Covenant leadership, based in its capital, Legacy, had never wanted the barren lands of the North, anyway, simply because they are worthless, and the cost of making a final push north would have been too high. Also, another threat appeared, that not even the Janissaries could contain alone."

Dave cocked his head. He'd never heard of this.

"Far to the west, even further than we are now, lies the Rift. A deep depression created by the Fall that separates the furthest reaches of the Covenant from a wasteland far more dangerous than anything found up north. A poisonous river runs through the Rift, creating a natural barrier, and sheer cliffs rise on both sides of this depression. Beyond the Rift, there are people, descendants of other survivors of the Fall, but very different. Disease and radiation have turned them into aggressive predators, fighting amongst themselves, scavenging. Some of the tribes are cannibals, others have turned to some sort of twisted religion, and human sacrifice is common." Dave shuddered.

"A zone was created, two hundred kilometers wide, between the Rift and the Covenant. A forbidden zone, where only a few select people, in Service to the State, would be allowed. These people would be rangers, soldiers, scientists, and independent thinkers who knew when to act and how. They would be sworn to secrecy, because the sights they would see out there, and the things necessary to do to protect our people, were something our leaders decided to spare the people of the Covenant. These were the first Wardens, and this camp is located inside that forbidden zone." Dave's heart skipped a beat, and he looked around. Others seemed surprised, as well, even Liz, who always seemed to take everything in stride, never letting anything faze her.

"When the first Wardens began patrolling the zone, there were still only Moon people officers in the Services. Eventually though, even the English had to be put in charge among the lower ranks, because the Moon people, though they have multiplied since the Descent, were only so many. And when disloyal Janissaries and Wardens revolted, it was English commanders who put down the revolt. In recognition of their Service, Covenant leadership decided to extend the privilege of citizenship to all who serve honorably to their term's end. Also, because of the mortality rates among the Janissaries, the term was reduced to three years instead of the usual seven. A good many other laws were passed in the final year of the second Covenant. So many that by year's end, the third Covenant was proclaimed. Among the new laws was the creation of the Students, the Service where the University and the Academy would select the very brightest young men and women to be groomed into scholars." It still stung. Dave knew he should have been among the Students, although he'd fit in just fine here in the Wardens. But still, the way the lecturer had just described Warden Service, he now felt a pang of regret, for not being up in Legacy, with Chas and Felicia.

"For thirty years, there was peace, and then the first Corpus revolt happened. It was put down hard, and ever since, life in the Corpus has remained... well, let's just keep it at that. Corpus Service is a sacrifice, something that someone must do for the common good of all the rest of us. Those who manage three years in the Corpus are usually transferred from mining and farming to factory work, which is a bit better. Still hard work, but those working the factories have earned the right to better conditions. I'll put it this way, in the factories, there are foremen instead of whippers." The Warden seemed to have eased into his lecture a bit more, and it seemed less of a recital, now that he was approaching modern times. The initiates also seemed a bit more eager. Now and then, a question would arise, and the Warden would try to answer as best he could.

"Why do those people on the other side of the Rift try to come here?" someone asked.

"Well, there may be several reasons, but I suspect life out there can be pretty unbearable. Unfortunately, disease and radiation have mutated their genes so badly, we cannot allow them to pass the zone. So we stop them. Sometimes we have to fight them and sometimes we just help them return to where they came from. Next question?"

"Does anyone ever go the other way?"

"No, or at least, they won't get too far. We have motion detectors and sensors all over the zone, and if someone should enter from the east, they will be turned back.

The zone is forbidden. The Rift is something only a Warden should see. And the wastelands beyond, well, I wouldn't want anyone to go there. Crossing the Rift is death. Next!"

"What caused the Rift?"

"The Fall. Or rather, the thing that caused the Fall. Next."

"What caused the Fall?"

"A disaster. Only the Moon people know the details. Only the Moon people are allowed to know. Next."

"The Moon people come from the Moon, right? What were they doing there?"

"I am not privileged to that information, and neither are you." Dave noticed the questions were taking a turn away from the history lesson, and the lecturer seemed to tighten up by it, like he wasn't supposed to talk about some of these issues. Warden initiates all seemed to be like him—curious, and although this line of questioning was interesting enough, Dave wanted to know more of the history.

"What happened after the first Corpus revolt?" Dave asked. The lecturer looked almost relieved at the question, and eager to answer.

"Well, when the Corpus first revolted, the third Covenant was deemed to have come to an end. After that, the leadership decided there would only be one "Covenant," where new laws and orders could simply be incorporated into the old system." He paused for a moment, thinking hard.

"Once the first revolt was put down hard, you would have expected there to be a long period of peace. But the opposite happened. The third Covenant ended seventy-one years ago, and in the first fifty years, there were three major uprisings. Now, this is classified information, not to leave Warden territory, you got that?" He waited until everyone either nodded or answered yes, before continuing.

"All evidence point toward outside involvement. That makes it different from the revolts of the past, which have all come from within the Covenant. The last three were instigated from the outside. Which poses a difficult question: who had the capability to threaten the Covenant?"

"Savages from the North?" someone asked. The lecturer made a gesture.

"Who knows? Could be that, or someone from the less damaged populations out west. They do have weapons out there, you know." He shrugged.

"Either way, the last revolt was more than twenty years ago, and the Covenant has been very prosperous since then. Nowadays, I don't see an uprising as a likely thing to happen. The economy is good, the Corpus seem quiet, the Janissaries are in control of the northern borderlands, and we have noticed nothing unusual out here. A few intrusions now and then, but they are swiftly dealt with, and it doesn't seem organized in any fashion. No, I'd say this is a good time to serve, and hopefully you'll all earn your citizenship in a time of peace and prosperity." Dave couldn't agree more. As long as there was peace, he would deal with the challenges his Service would throw at him. But as the lecture ended, he wondered if his time of Service would be as quiet and uneventful as the lecturer had expected, or if the last fifty years had just been the calm before the storm.

Chapter 4

MARK

He was late for his meeting with Head Servant Lunde, and should have been in a hurry. Instead, he took his time dressing after a long and invigorating shower. He figured Head Lunde would put up with it; after all, if not for Counselor Mark Novak's mind, Lunde would be long dead, along with his wife and all of his mistresses, his children, and his children's children. Come to think of it, the head servant's children's children's children would probably be long gone, as well. He chuckled without mirth.

No, Moon people or not, everyone waited for Mark Novak.

He turned toward the mirror and looked at his face. Once, it had been a young man's face, and one women tended to fall for. Although it rarely changed much these days, it had been a long time since his face had the features of a young, successful scientist and womanizer. His ice blue eyes still had that particular twinkle, and his hair, long, blond, and slicked back, showed not a single grey hair. Still, he could see where youth had lost, not to age, but rather agelessness.

He looked closer, putting a finger up near his right eye. A wrinkle forming. Crow's feet. He exhaled deeply. It would be time for another treatment soon. Months of isolation, cryo sleep for weeks at a time, while the doctors worked their magic.

His magic.

He had long abandoned performing procedures himself, but he still worked on perfecting the small parts, all those little details, whenever he felt like doing a little work. Not that he needed to; it was just something he liked doing now and then, whenever his need to feel useful threatened to overwhelm him.

He wondered for a moment if he should call for a pleasure lady and some stimulants for after the meeting, but decided against it. He usually felt more tired afterward, and with another treatment coming up, he knew he needed all the energy he could muster. Besides, it just made him feel more empty, the kind of empty only someone as privileged as he would ever experience.

He looked away and put on his slippers. He should be grateful. The Moon people had given him everything in return for the treatments and his advice. He was a trusted citizen, a hero respected by everyone. The one who witnessed the Fall. The one who dealt the final blow to a dying nation, clearing the way for the Moon people to come into their right. The one who gave every citizen the chance to live forever. Or as close to it as anyone could possibly know, given that he was the oldest man in the world. The one who enabled the reign of the Moon people through the power of life itself.

Something gnawed at him, though; this constant feeling of... wrong.

That everything about this was so very, very wrong.

He had been a rebel once. He even brought his best friend into it, and look where that got him. His friend died, a broken man fallen from grace, held captive in a prison cell somewhere. And though Mark eventually got his revenge, in hindsight, it all looked pointless.

No, he was done rebelling.

Leaving his luxurious apartment felt good. It was but a few minutes' walk to the Palace, but he enjoyed the vigor and bustle of Legacy. Although most people here, at least those visible to him, never had to work, they still seemed busy with some thing or another. If he managed to suspend disbelief for a few moments, it felt almost like walking through a prosperous city in the old world.

Almost.

He hardly noticed as he walked straight through the gates and up the walk to the Palace entrance. The Moon Palace Guard officer on duty saluted him, but Mark hardly acknowledged his presence. As the doors opened, he strode through the great reception hall. Everyone he met knew him by sight and moved out of his way. He ignored everyone as he walked to the elevator leading up to the apartments occupied by Head Servant Lunde.

Once the elevator stopped, he exited, and entered the head servant's office, which took up the outer part of his apartments. The room was lavishly decorated, with gilded ornaments everywhere, in addition to the white and black of the Moon people covering the walls and ceiling. The carpet, oddly, was a deep crimson, and only a few people knew the symbolism. All of them Moon people, except for Mark Novak. Earth history from before the Fall was banned from non-citizen schools, and nothing of Moon history before the Descent was taught to English kids, either. And while most Moon children had learned of the Youth Revolution by the first grade, the grisly details were a long forgotten chapter. But he knew.

"Ah, there you are, Counselor," Head Servant Lunde said, rising from his chair behind the enormous oak desk. He motioned for Mark to follow him over to the lounge chairs in front of the ancient fireplace, an artifact salvaged from the ruins of the house of the last president before the Fall. Mark thought it fit right in here, although, he mused, Lunde probably didn't even know that president's name. He held back a chuckle. Mark knew.

"You look tired, friend. Is it time again?" Mark

nodded.

"No way around it."

"Well, don't hold off for too long. Everyone depends on you, Novak."

"Yeah... Although I guess there would be plenty of people ready to take my place if I didn't take it this time."

"Don't speak like that," Alexej Lunde said, a frown interfering with his otherwise perfect features. *Movie-star face*, Mark thought. *Too perfect*. He half-smiled.

"Don't worry. It's just an old man's grumbling," he said.

"Well, you are old." The head servant's frown turned into a grin. "But I guess you are entitled to grumble." He snapped his fingers, and a hologram appeared before them, showing a model of the continent. *Still so strange*, Mark thought, *to know that most people, citizens or not, would never see that image. They would only see the smaller version, the one showing less than a fourth of this.*

"The Covenant," Head Lunde said, as the model morphed into a three-dimensional map seen from a bird's point of view, with the Covenant in white, the border in black, and everything else a dull brown.

"Surrounded by enemies. The coast held clean for the last century, thanks to the battleships and our orbital stations. The land border, though..." He shook his head. "We control the northern border, as we have for so long, although who knows what is brewing up there. The savages are a nuisance, but no real threat. Cannot even speak properly."

"French," Mark said, "or rather what used to be French. Evolved."

"I know, and you know that I know," the head servant snapped, "but it's a brute's language. Primitive." He sat back and moved his fingers to enhance the westernmost part of the Covenant on the map.

"The Rift, though. There have been more than a few episodes lately." Mark nodded. He'd seen this coming.

"Four years ago, it was the aircraft. Luckily, we had an orbital platform nearby and took it down before it reached visible airspace. Then, for the last two years, the number of incursions, both hostile and civilian, has increased. The Wardens consume twice the amount of Bliss now, compared to five years ago. The labs are hard pressed to keep up with demand. Some self-medicate because the latest version of Bliss tends to let fragments through from time to time, but kissweed or whatever they do these days, doesn't fix their perception. Dulls it a little, I guess, but without Bliss, everything would unravel." Mark nodded, impatiently.

"So what should we do about it, Alexej? Can we hold the Rift?" he asked.

"We need to ramp up production. More Corpus

initiates, more labs, longer hours. No way around it. We need more Bliss, a lot more. As it is, the dosages are pushed so low, someone could develop immunity or worse, total recall." The head servant paused, before he stared back at Mark, jaw set.

"Whatever we have to do, we will do it. The Moon people have always done whatever it takes. It is the will. To desire the means, as well as the end. We shall hold the Rift for a thousand years, Mark. A thousand years." Mark saw it as clearly as he ever had then. The will to rule, the determination to use any means necessary to achieve their goals. The legacy of the Moon people, forged in the Moon dust, a force that had led them back to Earth, and one day would make them rulers of the entire planet. He saw it and shuddered. And yet, he was part of it, for better or worse. He had chosen sides a long time ago, and he meant to see it through.

DAVE

"So, basically, the Covenant consists of two economic systems?" Dave asked rhetorically. Scientist Hughes nodded back at him. Dave was eager and had found that the Wardens, although not as prestigious and well known for their research and knowledge as the Students, were a Service where those who had a thirst for knowledge might find themselves well situated. The scientists were only too eager to welcome initiates such as Dave, who had barely missed Student Selection. One of them, Rogers, claimed that those picked by the Wardens often had stronger motivation than Student initiates, which made them better scholars in the long run. Dave had learned that while the Students had their Academy and their University, the Wardens had their Cottage. It wasn't well known, or glamorous in the least, but Dave was beginning to believe it might be equal to the Legacy institutions in quality of research and inventory of knowledge.

They had spent the first few weeks in camp, learning everything from how to build a fire and constructing improvised shelter, to physical training, to intermediate physics, chemistry, and economics. They had even learned the basics of handling a weapon. When they were deemed worthy, the initiates moved into the Cottage for a month of advanced learning. The scientists assessed each initiate individually, and Dave was among the first group to be awarded the honor. This was the first lecture at the Cottage he attended, and he immediately felt more at home with the more advanced levels of learning here, than with the more basic levels taught back at the initiate camp.

"Indeed, Initiate Wagner. How many of you have ever thought about why most people just sells their goods locally? Simple, it's a matter of price and demand. To move goods further than a few towns away would increase the cost of goods, making them too expensive to sell, and unable to compete with goods carrying lower transportation costs. So that limits the business geographically," Hughes said. Dave thought of how he had learned that all motor transport outside your allowed area was forbidden, and that trains and their cargo were controlled by the government in Legacy.

"So the people in Legacy, who get all their goods from the Corpus lands, though paying a higher transportation cost, actually pays less altogether because of the cheap labor," Dave said.

"Service. Not cheap labor. Service to the State," Hughes admonished mildly, a hint of a smile touching the corner of his mouth, before he addressed the class.

"But yes, a little blunt, but Initiate Wagner got it right. Those are the two economic systems we have in the Covenant. One that sustains a strong State and the welfare of its citizens, and one that ensures a sound economy, with an optimal distribution of goods among the non-citizens in every town from Charlestown in the south to Fort Winter in the north." He looked at his watch. Unlike school back home, there was no set time and no bell to signal the end of one class and the beginning of another. No, it was all up to the scientists. And there was plenty of time between classes for such a flexible system, time that the initiates spent discussing amongst themselves, asking follow-up questions to the scientists, or just hanging out with friends. Dave found that even though he had thrived in the more disciplined system back home, he actually learned more, or rather, he gained a deeper understanding of the subjects, within the Warden system.

"Time for a break, folks. Scientist Kasparov will be ready in half an hour, so let's try to stay close, shall we?" Everyone scurried out of the classroom, speaking loudly amongst themselves.

"Initiate Wagner. Will you stay for a few minutes, please?" Scientist Hughes said. Dave immediately froze. It must be something he said. He was terrified of messing up, now that he was beginning to think of the Wardens as so much more than just a second best option for his years of Service. He held back until everyone had left the room, standing a few steps away from Scientist Hughes, waiting nervously.

"David Wagner... Charlestown boy, right? We don't get too many from your parts..." He made a swiping movement on his infopad, and read quietly for a moment. Dave remained quiet.

"Hm. Such a clever young man. I bet you expected to be somewhere else right now though, didn't you?" The scientist sighed. Dave tried to think of something to say, but the words just wouldn't come.

"Well, there's not much glory or fame to be had here, so if that's what you were hoping for, I can assure you, life here will be difficult for you." He peered at Dave, cocking his head slightly to the left.

"But that's not it, is it? No, I don't think it is. You have something there, kid. Potential, yes that's it. You don't care about the fame and the prestige and all that, no… You seek knowledge. And such a seeker of knowledge can have a bright future here. Unless of course…" Hughes stopped abruptly. Then he smiled and closed the folder.

"The system isn't perfect, far from it. But it's the best we could possibly have. Before Descent and the Great Recovery, there was chaos. Before that, a system that in the face of danger, couldn't protect its citizens."

"But isn't it unfair that…" Dave began, but stopped when he saw the hard look the scientist gave him.

"The system prevents disorder. And yes, it rewards the citizens of Covenant. Understand this, though, Initiate Wagner: the State is vital to our survival. Citizens earn their privileges. And one day, you might, as well." He sighed again.

"You will learn, son. I wasn't born a citizen; I don't have Moon blood running through my veins. But I've learned that everything we have, our way of life, is all because of the Moon people, and the concept of Service to the State." Dave noticed Hughes got a faraway look in his eyes as he paused for a moment. Then he focused his gaze on Dave once again.

"There are dangers you wouldn't dream of out there, Initiate. If we were to give an inch, our enemies would take everything we've got. Everything we've built. And ultimately, we would be left outside of the protection of the Moon people." Dave nodded slowly. He knew there were dangers outside the safety of the Covenant. He'd never taken most of it seriously, though. It had always felt too distant. Hughes, on the other hand, looked like he knew more than he would tell, and yet, he obviously felt the need to warn Dave. To make him take it as seriously as he did.

"The Moon people saved us all, and every day since, the Covenant has been all about preserving what they built. Moon blood or not, we're all in this together." The scientist's stare seemed to pierce right through him, and Dave saw something he hadn't noticed before. Fear. Like he'd seen more than was good for him. And a fervor Dave hadn't noticed before. He felt a chill running down his spine.

"We're living on the edge of a knife's blade, son. One wrong move, and our society falls. We are Wardens, and our job is to make sure that doesn't happen. Whatever the cost."

As Dave walked toward his next lecture, he had a feeling he'd soon enough learn what Scientist Hughes seemed to fear so much. And he didn't look forward to it.

SUE

She was breathing heavily, every breath misting in front of her, fogging up the visor for a split second before the nano bots cleared it again. Autumn had arrived, and the leaves on the trees were changing into red and orange hues. And although the days were still warm enough, the mornings were steadily becoming colder. Inside the battle dress, she was comfortable, though. The AI regulated the temperature and let moisture out through vents, keeping her warm and dry. A few hours ago, she had felt a jolt of energy as the suit had injected a small dose of caffeine into her system, but the effect was now long gone. The adrenaline of being out on her first patrol had worn off, as well. For three days, they had been walking, with just two hours of sleep. And not a sign of the northerners, except a few run-down huts that Tac Hordvik had explained were the remains of an enemy settlement that had been terminated years ago. "Too close to our borders," he had said and continued to explain that no settlements south of the river were allowed. That would be too risky. Not that he had needed to tell any of them. It was all part of basic training, learning about their enemy and the rules of engagement.

Now, she was beginning to look forward to returning

to camp. She had expected combat, but Tac had explained beforehand that the savages often fled instead of fighting them, especially since the patrol would never penetrate the deep woods. In a couple of hours, they would reach the exfiltration point, where they would be picked up by an armored airship. Once they returned to camp, they would march through the grounds still wearing the battle dress, to be treated with a lavish dinner. On such occasions, it was not uncommon that one of the strategos or some other high official would come and join them, share the meal with them, and talk to them almost as equals. Survivor night, it was called, and it was one of the traditions the Janissaries kept, a rite of passage of sorts. Whether shots had been fired or not, they would then be full Janissaries, no longer mere initiates.

Sue was jolted from her thoughts by a whisper inside her helmet. It was Keisha, who covered the left flank with Brad. She looked over and saw they had already raised their weapons, ready to fire at anything. Sue, on the opposite end, raised hers, as well, covering the right flank with Quinn. She didn't like him, but they were teammates, and whatever personal issues they had disappeared as they worked together as limbs of the same body. Julian, front man for today, had taken a knee and held a hand up to his helmet, signaling activity in front of them, as well. Tac Hordvik, positioned a little to the back, centered, looked over his shoulder and gave a signal for Sue to leave the right flank and strengthen the front with Julian. They had trained for this, and Sue noticed the movements came naturally to her as she quietly slipped behind Quinn's firing zone to take up position with Julian. The six-man patrol, though green, was a cohesive fighting unit now, ready to move against whatever came their way, and Sue felt the rush of adrenaline as the AI injected a stimulant into her veins. Her breath became deeper, her focus clearer, and all signs of fatigue disappeared in an instant. Even her vision improved; the contrasts became clearer, and her eyes seemed to receive more light, enabling her to see things that normally would be hidden by shadow.

"Contact, ten o clock, two hundred meters," she heard Keisha's voice say in her helmet. The voice was steady and calm. She looked over and saw what had previously been hidden. A camouflaged blanket, probably heat resistant so the AI wouldn't notice, hid several shapes, stirring.

"Three seconds," Tac Hordvik said, just as calmly. Sue moved her weapon slightly, so not to alert the enemy.

"Two." She tensed.

"One." She threw her weapon up to her shoulder, initially not bothering to aim. It was all about overwhelming the enemy at first.

"Engage." The deafening roar of automatic weapons, the explosions of smart rounds, one in every ten, the screams of their enemy as they realized they were under attack. It only took half a second before the sound was adjusted to comfortable levels by the AI, and she wondered what it must be like for the northerners.

"Baseline left," she heard Tac Hordvik say, louder, but still calm and systematic. He had been under fire before, and she was glad to have someone like him leading now. Sue and Julian moved just as they had trained for so many times, while Quinn on the right flank would be moving behind them all and taking up position to the left of Tac Hordvik. She was relieved that fear didn't stop her from doing everything just as they had trained. Then again, it might be something the AI gave her.

Seconds later, the team was lined up, side by side, spaced two meters between each of them, still firing at where the enemy had shown itself. So far, so good.

"One forward," the tacticus said. She moved forward, while counting. One, two, three, four, five. Down on one knee, firing in bursts. Julian, to her right, fitted another hundred-shot magazine into his weapon. She still had sixty left in hers, so she waited. Keisha, on her left didn't change hers, either.

"One covering," Keisha said.

"Two forward," Tac Hordvik said. It was all just as they had practiced, everything moving smoothly, taking the battle to their enemy within seconds. Sue, Keisha, and Julian firing everything they had, while Quinn, Hordvik, and Brad moved steadily forward.

"Two covering," she heard Hordvik say as they took a knee to their left, returning to the perfect line. Sue quickly ejected the almost empty magazine, sticking it to the suit, where magnets would keep it in place for later. A fresh magazine went into her weapon, and she was ready again. Keisha was eyeing her, having done the same.

"One forward," came another command. She leaped up and moved forward. One, two, three, four.

A loud blast from the back made her stumble and fall.

Chapter 5

DAVE

Dave had loved the days at the Cottage. He felt like he had stuffed his head with knowledge, everything from economics and history to math and physics. And still he craved more. He was delighted by the fresh perspectives and noticed that, rather than rote learning, the Warden scientists encouraged curiosity and free thinking. They encouraged initiates to question the truth and what the scientists taught. There were limits, such as whenever someone questioned by which right the Moon people ruled, or what lay beyond the Rift, but except for the obvious taboos, the everyday discussions tended to be enlightening.

Back at the camp, the learning centered more around practicalities, and though he liked those parts, as well, he often found himself longing to return to the Cottage. He had begun to consider his specialty and knew that he had a decent chance of becoming an assistant scientist or maybe a techie, both paths that, given time and hard work, could lead to scientist positions at the Cottage. He lifted his gaze from the textbook, *Intermediate Materials Technology*, and looked out at the quiet part of camp where he had sat down next to a thick tree trunk to study. A couple of initiates were studying nearby, engaged in hushed discussion over something on their infopads. A Warden, a few years older than Dave, was telling a small group of initiates a tall tale, with the initiates staring wide-eyed at him. Two other Wardens were smoking, their futile attempts to suppress their giggles only making them look all the more stupid. *Kissweed*, he thought.

Discipline among the Wardens was generally lax, completely different from what he had expected. Compared to school back in Charlestown even. It normally suited him just fine. He couldn't imagine himself surviving the strictness of Janissary life, or the back-breaking Corpus serfdom. He had a hard time understanding why the Covenant needed such an institution as the Corpus, but every time he mentioned it, the scientists would tell him it was necessary to preserve the integrity of the Covenant. And though he didn't fully agree, he understood their reasoning. Also, he knew there were things he wasn't told, and that only as a full citizen would he be privy to some of the secrets that the Moon people held back from the English, and that everything would make sense to him one day. Once he learned the truth.

There were some aspects of the lax discipline he didn't like as much, though. He had noticed already on his first day in camp that Wardens openly smoked kissweed. Few initiates did, but as far as he could tell, almost every seasoned Warden did from time to time. He shook his head. He couldn't imagine how otherwise bright young people, citizen prospects, with an eternity of discovery ahead of them, would consume something that would dull the senses, and over time make you as dim as the neighborhood drunk.

He turned his eyes away, trying to concentrate on the subject at hand. He enjoyed the lectures, and he had a knack for learning, something the scientists were already noticing, he knew. But as he sat there, focus seemed to elude him. He kept thinking about what was soon to happen. The Wardens were tasked with protecting the Covenant from what lay beyond the Rift. As much as it was the reason for their existence, it was something no one discussed in detail. Whenever a discussion touched upon this, the final words were something along the lines of "You'll see" or "Give it time, you will learn soon enough." Dave had a hard time settling for that, but he knew he'd get no answers.

He had a few ideas, though. He'd heard talk of the infected. And the skirmishes and the patrols. And some of the older Wardens had a particular stare. As if they had seen things that were impossible to put into words. He knew there were some things you couldn't "un-see." And even if he got his choice of specialization, which would be far from physically demanding, front-line duty, he knew that every scientist, every steward had been out there at least once, and had seen whatever it was no one would talk about. That was the way of the Wardens. No one was to remain innocent. Everyone shared whatever burden they had to carry. Though he thought it sounded like a nice idea, he often wondered what it all meant. And there was something unsettling about it, as well. As if, once he crossed some particular line, there would be no going back.

SUE

Sue shook her head and wiped dirt from the outside of her visor. A scream pierced her ears from the helmet comms system, before it was muted. Brad. She glimpsed the enemy in front of her withdrawing, and turned half way around. Brad was lying on the ground, cut almost in half by the explosion. Dead or dying, it didn't matter. Even the fabled Janissary suit couldn't save him from such a blast. Quinn was also down and lay motionless. She saw Tac Hordvik crawling toward him, firing short bursts every few seconds. She couldn't see what he was aiming for, but she threw her weapon around and fired a long burst in the general direction he was firing, before getting up. She ran over to him, followed by Julian, while Keisha stayed back, covering their backs. There was a low dip in the terrain, where they would be safe from direct fire. At least for a little while.

"I've already called for backup," the tacticus said. "But unless we take out that rocket launcher, the airship will not come. They're not risking an airship for a bunch of green initiates." Sue could see he was gritting his teeth, and for a moment, she thought it was anger at their superiors who would sacrifice them so easily. But then, she saw where his suit had been penetrated. The nano bots were already covering the hole in the suit, just above the knee, but there was no hiding the blood soaking through.

"You're hurt," she said. He nodded.

"Yes, but the bots are stitching me up as we speak. Hurts like hell, though. AI won't give me anything but weak local anesthetic, either. Have to stay alert." She nodded, thought for a second, before she spoke.

"Tac, you stay here with Quinn and Keisha. Julian and I will take out the launcher." The tacticus stared at her and seemed about to say something. She cut him off, a bit too harsh.

"Tacticus, sir, we have no choice. You are incapacitated whether you like it or not. This is the only way." She didn't wait for an answer as she motioned for Julian to follow her.

"Now," she said, her voice calm, though her thoughts raced. She had just relieved her superior of command. If they survived, which was anything but certain, she could face dire consequences. Nevertheless, this was their only chance, and looking at the remains of Brad, she didn't think they'd get another.

Sue and Julian leapt from cover simultaneously, firing everything they had while they ran. The ammo in the magazines would only last for a few more steps. When she estimated they were down to the last twenty rounds, she shouted, a little too loud, for Julian to take cover. As soon as they hit the ground, she turned a switch on the side of her weapon, lifted it to point up in a 45-degree angle, and fired. A blast of heat passed to the side of her helmet. The heat-seeking missile should search out their attackers within seconds. She craned her neck to see, knowing she was exposed, waiting to see where the missile hit.

A blast just to the right of where she had expected it told her the location of their attackers. Both she and Julian took a knee, fresh magazines clipped onto their weapons, and blasted away. Fifty rounds each, give or take, before they stood up and moved forward, firing short bursts with every step. As they reached the tree line, she knew she would soon be out again. They both took a knee as soon as they stepped into the shade of the forest.

"Keep firing. I'll switch first," she said. Julian just nodded. Once she was done, he did the same, while she covered. Once they'd both reloaded, they moved forward again, slower now. After twenty or thirty meters, they came upon the remains of the enemy position taken out by the heat seeker. The dead lay strewn, and some sort of off-road vehicle still burned.

"Let's hurry. They can't be far away," she said. "The launcher must be slowing them down. See the mount?" She pointed at the burning vehicle. It had clearly been fitted with a weapon.

"Those weapons are powerful, but cumbersome. I can't believe they plan to carry it off," Julian said.

"Yeah, I guess they would have a hard time replacing it," Sue answered, knowing well that the northerners didn't have nearly the resources of the Covenant.

They ran through the forest, knowing that they could be running into an ambush at any time. But if they didn't take out the launcher soon, Quinn would be dead. And if that airship wouldn't come pick them up, they would all die.

The air was crisp, and outside of a few rays of light coming through the canopy of the forest, shadow covered the ground. The visors adjusted swiftly between light and dark, though, so Sue had no problem seeing.

"Careful," she heard Julian whisper inside her helmet as something snapped. She cursed quietly and pulled her foot from the broken branch. The enemy didn't have the equipment of the Janissaries, but they still had ears. She took a moment to look around. Nothing. Then they kept walking, a quick pace, but more careful with where they put their feet down. Julian took the front, while Sue tried to cover both sides. They needed to move fast, but if they came upon the enemy without the element of surprise, it would be two against who knew how many. And not even Janissary suits or their superior weapons could be relied upon to keep them alive through that.

~

After a few minutes, Julian stopped, raised his left fist, and took a knee, weapon raised and ready to fire.

"Twelve o'clock." Sue heard his voice, an amplified whisper. She took a knee and waited. After a few seconds that seemed to last an eternity, Julian lowered his hand, palm down and out to his left. Although even the barest whisper would be heard inside the helmets, using hand signs for when they preferred quiet was something Tac Hordvik had emphasized time and again. You never knew what the enemy heard, or what equipment they might have gotten their hands on. Sue crept carefully forward, taking up position a few meters left of Julian. They were almost ready.

They looked at each other, and Sue held up five fingers. Both made sure their spare magazines were within easy reach and pointed the right way. Everything to make time spent changing as short as possible. Four. Sue glanced through her scope and made a small adjustment for distance. The enemy was no more than sixty or seventy meters in front of them, dragging the heavy rocket launcher between them. One looked injured. Three. There seemed to be six or seven of them. With the element of surprise, Sue and Julian should be able to take them out swiftly. Sue was acutely aware that these would probably be hardened veterans, though. Two. She was green. So green. But training did count for something, and there was no better training than that of the Janissaries. One.

They fired simultaneously, and two enemies fell at once. Sue moved the barrel slightly and fired again. One more down. She heard Julian fire two quick bursts, and followed up with one of her own. Missed. One of the savages managed to get a burst off in their direction, and she heard a scream both through her helmet and from the outside.

"Shit shit shit!" Julian screamed as he dropped his weapon. Sue fired another burst, and the shooter fell to the ground. She looked at Julian, who had taken cover. He was clutching his hand, bleeding. The medics would fix that back in camp. Painful, obviously, but nothing serious. His weapon was done for, though. Now, she was on her own. She focused, leaving Julian with his injury. How many left?

A stray bullet almost got her, but the defense bots deflected it. The suit was designed to deflect or stop bullets, but it didn't always work, and some parts of the body were more difficult to cover than others. The helmet, though, had some of the best defensive capabilities, including nano bots that within a microsecond could merge into an almost invisible shield in the air, a centimeter or so outside the helmet itself, and deflect the incoming bullet. It would destroy the bots, but could save her life. It just had, and she gave a quick thanks to the now wrecked little invisible fellows that would have to be replaced once they got back. If they got back.

She moved a meter to her left, in order to make for a less obvious target. In a split second, she saw movement, and she raised her weapon and fired a long burst almost even as she was still lifting the weapon. She heard a scream, and another voice shouted something. A female voice.

Sue edged forward to have a closer look. There, pinned down in a small depression, Sue could see one leg sticking out. *Careless*, she thought, taking aim. A single shot, and another scream. She got to her feet and ran toward the enemy, hunched low, aware that she might be wrong, there might be others.

She stood above the woman, covering her with the rifle. The woman rolled over, wincing from the injury.

"Me tuer, meurtrier!" the woman said. She couldn't be older than Sue, but the wide eyes and scruffy hair did nothing to hide her contempt. Sue didn't know what to do. Clearly, they couldn't let her go. But they had strict rules that taking prisoners was to be avoided. But here she was, holding her weapon at a girl that could have been her sister or a friend back in Charlestown, and she couldn't simply shoot her. She had no idea what those words meant, but it didn't matter. She glanced over at Julian as he came walking toward them, hoping that he would come up with a solution.

It all happened in an instant.

The woman drew the sidearm from underneath her and pulled the trigger. Had she been steadier, more experienced perhaps, Sue would be dead. Instead, the shot went off a split second before the gun actually pointed at her, and Sue reacted instinctively. A three-round burst. The woman shook a couple of times before she fell silent, eyes still wide from the shock.

"Shit, that was close," Julian said. "Are you okay?"

Sue nodded, dazed. She had just killed five people. That was in addition to the five or so killed back by the tree line. And the last one was a woman her own age. A prisoner. Nausea was quickly building up.

"Hey!" she heard Julian say, distant at first. "Hey! Don't break down on me now, Sue. You did what you had to do. Let's just do what we came to do and get the hell out of here."

Sue could feel a calm coming that didn't seem completely natural. *The AI*, she thought, as her mind began to focus on the task at hand. She breathed deeply, and exhaled, the nausea gone and composure regained.

"You got a charge ready?" she asked. Julian nodded and tried to reach his pocket on his left side with his good hand. He fumbled a little, and Sue reached over.

"Let me," she said. Their eyes met, and she noticed his half-smile behind his visor. She looked away and reached into his pocket, grabbing the multi charge. She walked over to the rocket launcher, which looked intact still, with just a few small dents from the small-arms fire. She placed the charge beside the firing mechanism, so that it would inflict the most damage.

"Let's go," she said, keeping her eyes away from Julian's.

They walked for a couple of minutes, Sue in front, weapon ready. Just in case. Once Sue thought they were far enough away, they stopped. Sue took out a small controller unit and pressed a button. After a moment, a red light turned green, and she pressed the button again.

The blast wasn't as powerful as she remembered from training. But here, in these woods, all sounds were muffled by foliage. They waited for half a minute before resuming their walk. Neither of them spoke. Instead, Sue switched to team frequency.

"Two-One-Bravo, this is Two-Four-Bravo."

"This is Two-One-Bravo. You guys done yet?" Tac Hordvik answered.

"Affirmative. Any news on exfil?" Sue hoped the airship would be there in time to save Quinn and get them out before the enemy realized they had wounded Janissaries that would be an easy target if they came in force. The tacticus remained silent for a few seconds before replying.

"We have a go for exfil. So get your butts over here A.S.A.P., before the big shots decide to leave without you."

"Don't worry about us. We'll be there. Two-Four-Bravo out."

"You hear that?" she said to Julian.

"Yeah. Let's get a move on."

They ran as quickly as they could, and Sue worried that if an enemy spotted them, they would be defenseless. But there were no more enemies around, and they soon reached the clearing where the others were waiting, just as the airship arrived. Keisha ran a few meters off and began directing the airship as it lowered toward them. Once it hung just five meters or so above ground, a cage that looked like a cross between a basket and an elevator was lowered. Two heavily armored airmen, sporting some fancy weaponry Sue didn't recognize, leapt out and covered the Janissaries. Two medics lifted Quinn onto a stretcher and carried him into the cage. Julian followed right behind, clutching his damaged hand.

"Shouldn't we pick up Brad?" she said to Tac Hordvik, who looked like he was about to fall over from blood loss. He just shook his head.

"He's gone, either way, Atlas. Care for the living." Keisha came running, and Sue followed her in. Once his team was inside, Tac Hordvik ushered the airmen to follow, and he got in last. The cage quickly rose up inside an opening in the belly of the airship. The doors underneath them banged shut, and they exited the basket and strapped themselves into seats in the back.

Once the airship picked up speed, Sue finally let herself relax. She took off her helmet and laid her head back. She was restless, though, and she could feel her hands begin to shake. No magic injections from the AI this time, now that she wasn't in any immediate danger.

Her mind was racing. Could she have done anything differently? How would the tacticus feel about her taking charge back there? Why did that woman have to draw that gun on her? What if she had disarmed her properly in the first place, would the woman be alive now? She had killed people…

Tac Hordvik scooted over to sit beside her. She could see he was in pain and wondered why he hadn't received any painkiller meds yet. They sat quiet for a moment, and she was the first to break the silence between them.

"I'm sorry, Tac. I shouldn't have run off like that. Injury or no injury, you are still my superior…"

He waved her off.

"You did well out there, Atlas. If not for your quick thinking, we'd still be down there, and Quinn would be dead for sure. For an initiate, you sure did raise hell today." He grinned, as she blushed.

"Okay… Are you sure, I mean, Tac…" He shook his head.

"What you did out there today took a lot of courage. You did the right thing, even though it could have cost you, had you pulled that on someone else. Me, I don't care about any of that." He smiled again and offered his hand. She took it and returned his firm grip.

"Oh, and Sue, my first name isn't Tac. It's Evan. Evan Hordvik." Sue laughed softly. The day had been so full of loss and hardship, but in the end, she had gained a new friend.

Chapter 6

MARK

Every time he visited in an official capacity, he tried not to wince when the locals tried to impress him. To be honest, he wasn't an easy man to impress. After all, if he hadn't seen it all, no one had. So he smiled and nodded as he exited the airship and stepped onto solid ground. The flags and fanfare, the ranking officers, the honor guard... It was all background noise to him. To be endured, so that he could do what he had come for. To get an impression of the state of the northern defenses, to see for himself how things were, unpolished and rough, and so much more reliable than the reports they received back in Legacy.

He'd been to Camp Sharpe before, but the visit he was thinking of as he walked on the concrete airpad was the one he'd made before the Fall. The memory that was so old, it was hard to distinguish from fantasy, but some details were vivid enough to make him forget that it had been more than two centuries ago. He'd been with his girlfriend at the time, a cute little thing called Wendy. He chuckled. There had been a few, back when he was quite the eligible bachelor. But he'd really believed in that relationship, for a while, and taken her to this place, which had been known to be a romantic hotspot. The waterfalls had impressed him, and it was sad to know that none of these youngsters would ever see what he'd seen. Even the lakes had disappeared. But some things hadn't changed. This was still on the border of this country. And even if it wasn't the same country anymore, it was still his.

The small group approaching consisted of three newly minted Janissaries and one tacticus, all sworn to protect this northern border, and his way of life. He could see their commander, a tacticus of Moon blood, walked with a limp, although he seemed to try not to. Another wore an oversize bandage on his right hand. Two girls. Women, he corrected himself. Unharmed, from the looks of them. The last one lay on a stretcher, carried off by medics, to be taken to the camp hospital. *Too bad*, Mark thought. He would have liked to shake his hand.

The man walking beside him, Sub Strategos Janev, the commander of Camp Sharpe and a twenty-year veteran of Janissary training, beamed as the small group stopped in front of them, coming to attention as one.

"Tacticus Hordvik. I see you brought these fine young Janissaries safely back from quite a skirmish," Janev said. He looked over at the one leaving the platform. "And from what I heard, that one over there will be just fine in a few weeks also. Well done." He shook the younger man's hand. The tacticus hesitated, and Mark thought he looked like he wanted to say something.

"Speak up, son, what is it?" Mark said. The tacticus, Hordvik, looked at him, and his eyes widened. Mark almost sighed. It was the same every time people realized who he was. The young man didn't hesitate for long though.

"It's, well, I don't deserve this, sir," he said. The sub strategos laughed, about to wave it all off as modesty, but the tacticus spoke again.

"This woman deserves the credit, sir. When pinned down and under fire, she single-handedly took out five enemies and a tactical rocket launcher. That was after she and this man incapacitated a nest of enemies that was about to slaughter us all. If not for her, none of us would be alive now." Mark looked at the young woman, who was blushing from the praise. She had long, dark hair, tied up in a knot, hazel eyes, and a look about her that told him this wasn't any ordinary youngster, picked up to serve and die. This woman was leadership material, and there was something there that he recognized instantly. A willingness to do the right thing, no matter the cost. He cocked his head slightly.

Sub Strategos Janev grinned.

"I promise I'll read the report, Hordvik, and if it is as you claim, I believe we have a distinguished merit under fire medal coming, don't you?" He laughed and turned to Mark.

"Not bad for a green initiate on her first combat

patrol. I told you we're training some fine young Janissaries up here, Counselor." Mark smiled back, eyeing the young woman sideways. She was staring straight ahead.

"You can say that again, Janev. I'm impressed." He hesitated for a moment. "I'm told you have a tradition here, when initiates become full Janissaries…"

"Oh, yes, Survivor Night. Well, it's not much to someone like you…" Janev said. Mark pressed on.

"I would very much like to join these fine young men and women. In fact, I was planning to ask you for a favor, but I understand it is custom that a high-ranking officer attends." Janev looked puzzled. Mark smiled. In order to get foot soldiers talking, he usually tried to get the officers out of the way.

"Now though, while you gather the information I need, I could take your place at this… dinner. I would love to get a chance to speak to them, and this way, you get the work done faster." He didn't wait for a reply. Whatever Mark Novak decided, a mere sub strategos would obey. Even if the blustering Janev was Moon people and he was not. Mark motioned for his attendants to follow, as he walked toward the suites prepared for him. Sub Strategos Janev remained standing for a moment before following.

Obedient dog, Mark thought. *Born to rule and all that.* He wondered what it would take, for someone with the power to make some real decisions, to see as he did that the system needed reform, or it would fall. The way things were heading, the Covenant wasn't sustainable. It reminded him too much of the systems he'd read about in history books, back in the old world. Systems that exploited the many for the gain of the few. A part of him wished for reforms, while another part secretly wished for the system to come crashing down. The one thing that frightened him, though, every time these thoughts came to him, was that if the latter happened, he would certainly be among the first to fall.

SUE

Ever since she first arrived at Camp Sharpe, Sue had heard talk of Survivor Night. Indeed, every Janissary who had passed their final test for their JJ bar, whether that was actual combat or not, had been through this. And now it was her turn. She was marching slowly beside Tac Hordvik. Behind her, Keisha and Julian followed. It was more of a leisurely walk than a march, but such was the custom on Survivor Night.

There were other patrols, as well, and she recognized Laurie from back home limping in the back of one of the patrols. So, he was one of those who would enter true Janissary status with combat experience. Others, who clearly hadn't seen combat, were staring at them, big-eyed and curious, although they looked weary, as well. The officers made sure no one got it the easy way.

Sue was acutely conscious that she must smell awful. No one was allowed to shower before Survivor Night—another Janissary tradition. They would wear their battle dress, complete with sweat, dirt, even blood, making the contrast to all the luxury even starker. The mess, usually nice enough but nothing lavish, would be decorated for the occasion.

Sub Meridian Hoston received them at the entrance. Although dirty from being out in the field with one of the patrols, he still looked like he had groomed himself, just a little. He had dark blond hair, short in the neck and on the sides, while the top had grown long enough to fall down on one side. He was probably around thirty, sporting a short, purple-dyed goatee that emphasized his grey eyes. Sue had seen him around camp, mostly just talking to the tacticus, passing down orders. Initiates never spoke to officers, and officers rarely bothered with initiates. Come to think of it, Sue had never seen him smile before, but now he did, a wide grin, ear to ear. He nodded to Tac Hordvik, who moved aside while Hoston opened a dark wooden box. Sue strained to see.

The box contained at least twenty small gold bars. The single bar of a Junior Janissary. The sub meridian pinned a gold bar to the lapel of her shirt first.

"Welcome, Janissary Atlas. May you reap honor," he said, right fist to the heart, Janissary style. Sue repeated the salute.

"We reap what we sow. Service to the State," she replied.

As soon as every member of her patrol had received their gold bar, they were let inside.

Sue stopped just inside, jaw agape. The mess was barely recognizable, and if she hadn't known better, she would have believed this was one of those fine restaurants she had heard of, one of those found only in the big cities, or even just in Legacy itself.

Cloth draped the walls, the black and white of the Covenant, and the floor was covered in red carpets. She felt guilty for stepping on such fine fabric with her muddy boots. There were candelabras lining the walls, and the tables were set with delicate white tablecloths, with a long black cloth dividing it along the middle, with thick candles burning. In front of every chair, the tables were set with fine silverware. And the smell! She noticed the servants lined up by the far wall holding large, covered trays. She didn't even know they had servants here in Camp Sharpe, but these looked like they had never done anything else their entire lives.

The headwaiter stepped forward and motioned for

them to sit down, and Sue hesitantly took a seat beside Keisha, who was quick to pick her place. Tac Hordvik—Evan, she reminded herself—sat down on the other side. The servants began to serve the first course, a fish of some kind. It was red and cold and salty, and melted on the tongue. The fruit laid beside it was something she had never seen before. It tasted heavenly, though. It was far too little, and her stomach growled as soon as she finished off the last bite.

A door on the far side of the room opened, and when she saw who entered, she laid down her silverware, swallowing hard. Counselor Novak smiled as he sat down opposite her. A servant offered to serve the fish, salmon he called it, but the counselor declined. How could anyone decline such food? He took some wine instead, smelling it thoroughly before he sipped.

"So, Atlas. I'm looking forward to hearing your story," he said, before turning toward Tac Hordvik.

"But first, tacticus, I must say I'm curious about you. I've heard very good things about you. The sub strategos tells me you have declined advancement more than once." Hordvik didn't say anything, and the counselor took another sip of his wine. He did something curious, which to Sue sounded like a gurgle. Then he swallowed, closing his eyes for a moment.

"Very nice…" he murmured, giving the headwaiter an

approving nod. Then he looked back at the tacticus.

"Evan Hordvik, a tacticus in the Janissaries, risking his neck again and again, instead of taking command like his father would expect of him. Declined a placement on Strategos Command two years ago, refused to go to the Military Academy one year ago—again, since you had the opportunity three years ago, as well. Made your father very angry when you decided to stay with the Janissaries even after he got you a placement with the Luna Brigade. Now that was one choice I never did understand. Some people, myself included, who believed you had an urge to be in the best combat unit, expected you to embrace that placement. I thought perhaps the challenge would tempt you. Even you would have struggled to be accepted through their selection process." Sue didn't understand half of this, but she did understand that Hordvik had had several opportunities that most wouldn't even dream of, and yet, he had chosen to remain with the Janissaries, a mere tacticus, when he could have been an officer a long time ago.

Sue almost didn't notice the servants placing the next course before her, until the smell woke her. The deer steak—from the preserve, obviously—with carrots, potato puree, and a creamy sauce made her mouth water, and she had a hard time restraining herself. The counselor noticed, though, and smiled as he motioned for her to eat.

"Go on, Janissary, eat. You have deserved this." She didn't wait for him to repeat, and took a bite. The meat was like nothing she had had back home. So tender.

"So, Hordvik. Why would someone of the Moon people, especially someone from a prominent family like the Hordviks, choose to serve with the Janissaries? And to continue serving for years. You know what you are risking. You're not like these kids from Charlestown or Holstonhead or Nevayrk. They don't have as much to lose. Thirty more years, against the possibility to live forever, what's that really, in the great scheme of things? But you are a Hordvik. So why?" Sue noticed the Evan's eyes narrowed. It was as if she saw two equals speaking, making her acutely aware of her own status.

"You mean, why I choose to serve?" Hordvik said. Novak nodded.

"Why shouldn't I serve?" Hordvik asked, giving the counselor a challenging stare. "Why shouldn't I?" The counselor cocked his head, just a little. Sue remembered seeing his face on television, years ago. She couldn't have been more than five or six years old. He looked exactly the same, except for the intensity of his eyes, never blinking. Television really didn't convey every detail.

"Okay, I get it. You choose to serve. But what about command? A strategos serves just as a tacticus does. But you choose to remain a foot soldier. Why?" Sue took another bite, but even the savory food couldn't distract her from the intensity of the conversation. Tac Hordvik eyed her, as if wondering whether to speak with an audience, but got a hard look as he turned his gaze back to the counselor.

"Service to the State. What does it really mean, Counselor?" He shook his head. "It has become empty words among my people. Why are we born citizens? Why are we automatically chosen for command? Those not of the Moon people; I've seen so many Janissaries from those small towns you mentioned, capable, intelligent people. Some of them are dead now. Others have chosen to extend their Service. Others again, are citizens today. They have earned it." His voice was ice now, but Sue noticed a slight movement, as if the counselor was nodding. *Curious*, she thought. Horvik didn't seem to notice, though.

"I was lucky," he continued. "I was born to rule… But here's the thing, Counselor. I think it corrupts us." He paused, only to speak again when Counselor Novak didn't say anything. "It corrupts the people, the State, everything. And if we don't change, the Moon people will fall. The Covenant will fall. Make no mistake, Counselor, I love my people, and I love the Covenant. I cannot stand idly by and watch the corruption eat away everything we have created since the Descent." He exhaled and seemed to notice the others staring at him. He picked up his glass and took a deep swallow. Then he grinned, setting his glass back down.

"So, in my small way, I choose to do what everyone should be doing. I serve."

Sue hadn't been wrong, the counselor was indeed nodding. The conversation between the two was clearly over, though, and the counselor turned his attention to her.

"Janissary Atlas, I would love to hear your story, and maybe the rest of you can help out, as well. Please, tell me what happened out there."

"I assume you've read the file, Counselor," she replied. Novak nodded affirmatively.

"Still, I'd like to hear your version of it. All of you." Sue took a deep breath—where to begin?

"Well, sir, let's begin with the first contact. I think Keisha was the first one to notice the ambush..." She continued by telling the story as thoroughly as possible. They all filled in whenever she became stuck, and Keisha gave a vivid description of how she had stormed forward, fearlessly, while the enemy was firing all over them. Too vivid for Sue's taste, and she'd never been fearless. Still the story told was mostly accurate, more than she would have been able to tell all by herself. She even told him about the woman, the prisoner. Julian took over when she began to speculate how she could have avoided killing her, for which she was grateful.

Sometimes Counselor Novak had a question, and she tried to answer as well as she could. In the end, Tac Hordvik told of their return and how the airship took them away, He repeated his claim that none of them would be alive if not for her actions.

"So, Susan, you relieved your superior of command. One of the Moon blood." There it was. The counselor hadn't missed that one point, that one fact that would be considered a serious crime, whatever else she had done. She felt her cheeks grow hot, but she didn't say anything.

"Sir, Counselor. She did what she had to do to keep us all alive," Hordvik protested. The counselor looked into her eyes, considering. Then he rose abruptly.

"Let's change that bit, shall we?" he said.

"Sir?"

"Let's not spread that part beyond this group. I'll fix the report; don't worry. And none of you tell that particular bit to anyone, got it?" He extended his hand, and she took it. His grip was firm, surprisingly so.

"We all know this was the only option, so let's just say that the tacticus gave the order, All right?" he said. Tac Hordvik grinned, and Novak grinned back.

"We all know that sometimes you have to break a few rules to set things straight," he said. Then he let go of her hand, turned, and walked out, leaving them all in silence. At last, Keisha broke the silence.

"Where is everyone? I thought Survivor Night was for everyone." Julian motioned for them to look over to the entrance from which they had come. The others were entering, led by Sub Meridian Hoston. Sue sat down again, hoping there was still some warmth in her food. Curious. The counselor must have made sure nobody else was around to hear her story. It was the only explanation she could think of. But why would he even care?

DAVE

The alarm pierced his ears and tore him out of sleep. Dave sat up, bewildered, and for a few seconds, he was back in Charlestown, wondering what was happening. Then, as he realized where he was, a chill ran down his spine. Could this be the real thing?

He got up and put on his pants. He pulled his shirt on, but messed up the buttons, so that one side of his loose shirt end hung lower than the other. He didn't bother to redo it. His boots went on, and he slapped the Velcro tight around his ankles. *Lucky they didn't use shoelaces*, he thought, as he sprinted out of the dorm with the others.

Just outside, two senior stewards stood handing out handguns and rifles to every initiate, before ushering them along. Dave got a pistol and was sent over to the next group of stewards, who were handing out ammunition. He got two boxes of cartridges and opened the lid slightly to look inside. Live rounds. So, if this was a drill, it was damn realistic.

Most Wardens didn't carry weapons in camp, just the ones who were on security duty, or certain senior positions. And the rangers. He saw one of the rangers, Harald something—Moon blood, obviously—in full combat gear, toting a scoped rifle and night vision goggles fastened to his helmet. Dave looked around at the other senior Wardens. Usually, they were a pretty cheerful lot, but now their faces were somber, serious. *This is it then*, he thought, *this is definitely no drill*. He went on to the great square set in the middle of camp, where everyone had their gathering points in case of an alarm.

"Sidnell," he heard someone shout, and then he saw Liz sprint by. He hadn't talked to her for a few days, since she began testing for ranger aptitude. Now, she looked like she was being outfitted for combat, and Dave shuddered. He hadn't chosen his specialization yet, but he had made no secret of wanting to enter tech or maybe science. He felt quite sure Liz would be chosen for the rangers, though. As far as he knew, she was just the kind they were looking for, whereas he was more the kind of Warden to end up in the Cottage.

A warden known to him only as Jared, and about one

year older, came over and stood beside him, looking at the group preparing for combat.

"See that, Wagner? They are taking initiates already. Usually, initiates are only brought along after at least six months," he said. Dave nodded. He'd heard.

"Looks like they are taking the ones singled out for ranger duty," he answered.

Jared got a faraway look.

"Yeah, thank the gods, or whatever. I hardly remember anything from my stint out there, but I do remember the fear and the feeling afterward. You'll see."

"Just… Just don't let it get to you, Dave, and you'll be fine." He forced a smile, and Dave noticed Jared swallow hard.

The rangers took off toward the airpad, taking Liz and at least five other initiates with them. The alarm stopped, and an older steward came over and told them they could go back to whatever they were doing. Jared wished him luck—tomorrow Dave would know which specialization he'd get—and took off. Dave walked slowly back to the barracks.

Although relieved, Dave wondered how Liz would fare. She was capable, no doubt, but something about the way nobody ever told him, or even seemed to remember any details, made him anxious.

The next morning, after a restless sleep, he went

straight to the square again. This time, it was no alarm, though. The initiates were gathered in the middle, where their assigned specialties would be announced, with spectators, people they had befriended, scientists, and senior Wardens, standing in small clusters around. No rangers, though, and none of the ranger initiates, either.

The man standing in front of the initiates was the same man who had greeted them when they had arrived by train, not two months ago. He had a different shirt this time, still colorful, though, and he didn't seem like he'd had a haircut or a shave since the last time Dave had seen him. His name was Gregor, and from what Dave had learned, he was head of everything around here, initiate training, operations, and all. He still didn't know his official title. But even through the shaggy exterior and the half-smile that never seemed to leave his face, Dave could tell this man was Moon blood through and through, even if he hadn't learned his name. He'd have been surprised if it had been otherwise, of course; nobody not of the Moon people would have been put in charge of anything of this size.

"All right, let's get on with this, shall we?" Gregor said. Dave noticed Brian standing nearby, and took a couple of steps to stand beside him. It felt right, to have another kid from Charlestown here to share the news with. Brian smiled as he noticed him, and then they both turned their attention to their superior.

"You should have noticed the absence of the ranger initiates. That's right, those selected to leave us last night have been accepted into ranger duty. Those of you who applied and didn't go, what can I say? Sorry, mates. We'll find you something more suitable." He grinned, while a couple of initiates standing among them shuffled and looked down.

The ranger initiates will receive most of their specialized training out in the field, although they will be living here until they are fully trained. And of course, some of them might be selected for instructor duty later on, and those you will see again." He paused for a moment, and though he seemed like he was thinking something funny, his eyes looked sharp as he eyed the initiates.

"As a matter of fact, they are on their way back now, and should be here any minute." Dave felt his heart beat a little faster. He couldn't tell whether it was fear of what could have happened to Liz and the others, or if it was the excitement of knowing that, in a few moments, he would receive his invitation into one of the specializations. He desperately hoped he wouldn't be picked for stewards or security. That would be a complete waste. And now that the rangers were out of the question, his ambitions were stirring again.

"Garret, Heineman, Wilson, Johnson, Callan,

Baldwin, Fredericks. You are to be trained stewards.

"Jefferson, Teller, Harrison, Greer, Billings, Ford, both Fords, actually... We'll have to work something out... Peterson, Scott, Desmond, Henderson, Bowers, Rollins. Security for you guys, and sorry about that comment. You are all to be Wardens, no matter what." Dave knew several of those chosen for security had applied for rangers, and though he knew the rangers were extremely selective, he'd thought at least one or two of them might make it. But like the commander said, they were all Wardens, first and foremost.

"Sawyer. You'll be an assistant scientist." Dave jumped. Brian to be a scientist? How could that be? Dave knew he was smarter and worked harder than Brian did. He didn't have time to brood though, as Gregor announced his name.

"Wagner. Tech for you." So, he would be a techie. *That wasn't too bad*, he thought.

He didn't pay attention as Gregor announced the rest. A small group to the engineers, who were essentially builders, and another group to medical. A group of six or seven who had to go through basic again, since their results weren't good enough for specialization. He almost didn't notice when Gregor congratulated them all and wished them luck. He'd learn every technology allowed, he would be sworn to secrecy and learn things nobody else was allowed to know. He'd have real career prospects. The brief envy over not being selected for scientist faded quickly; he'd learn so much more in tech, and once he'd served for a while, the Cottage would gladly welcome him. It would take a bit longer, but in the end, nobody in the Wardens, except Cottage scientists, knew as much as those in tech.

He was so caught up in his thoughts that he didn't notice the airship before it passed above him. *Liz*, he thought. He ran off toward the airpad, eager to tell her everything. When he approached, there were several others already standing there, watching as the rangers and their initiates disembarked. They all looked tired, and their uniforms were grimy. He noticed one of the initiates limped, while another had dried blood all over his legs. None of them seemed to notice the crowd, though.

Liz was one of the last to disembark. She seemed okay.

As she got close though, he saw her face. Her eyes. Her features were slack, and her pupils dilated. She seemed to stare at nothing, and when he greeted her, it was as if she stared straight through him. She looked empty.

"Let them through, guys. Come on, make room." That was Harald, the Moon-blood ranger. He didn't have the faraway look. On the contrary, he seemed alert and aware as he sternly made sure nobody got in the way. Dave stood aside and watched Liz and the others walk toward the hospital. A steward and a doctor, both Moon people he realized, let them in, and Harald closed the door briskly behind them.

"What happened?" Brian asked, as he came walking up, a big smile still on his face. Dave just shook his head.

"I really have no idea," he said. *Something isn't right*, he thought, and he instinctively knew he had to keep such thoughts to himself. *Something definitely isn't right.*

Chapter 7

DAVE

Dave loved it in Tech. He had never been able to learn so much before, and it turned out he had a real knack for it. He took apart drone consoles and rocket sighting systems. He learned how to repair communications systems. He began to study programming and electronics. He learned to file electronic folders in ways that made them invisible to everyone except those he chose to give access, and he learned to retrieve hidden files and crack secure systems. He even got to test it on their own systems.

"If we can break it, someone else could. This way, we stay on top of the development. Although, in reality, electronic warfare is a race which no one ever wins. The best you can do is stay one step ahead of your enemy." That was Senior Technician Hasle, his instructor and superior, around sixty and probably one of the oldest Wardens around. Come to think of it, he was one of the oldest people Dave had ever met. He was Moon people of course, but you wouldn't know it, except for his name. He looked nothing like the others, dark skinned and curly hair. Dave wondered if it would be all right to ask him about it, but deemed it inappropriate, so he let it go. Hasle treated him well from the first day. He let him take his time to get everything right, and whenever Dave had a question, Hasle would explain in a way that made him really understand what he was talking about.

He quickly understood there were areas of the system where even Hasle wouldn't let him test his skills, though. Once, when he suggested it, the older man had just laughed.

"I know you are talented, Wagner, but no matter how hard you try, that door will remain closed. Best not to think of it," he said.

When Dave brought up the subject a few weeks later, Hasle surprised him, by banging his fist on the table.

"I said let it go. You won't be able to do it. And even if you managed to, you'd regret it. Trust me." That was the only time he saw Hasle angry, and except for that one occasion, they got along fine.

While he was busy learning his new skills, he didn't have much contact with the others. He once saw Brian walking trough camp with Scientist Hughes, and then there was Liz.

She seemed changed, he thought. She wasn't around much, being out with the rangers most of the time, but she always made sure to check in with him whenever she wasn't out. Dave considered her his best friend here. Something was different about her, though. She was more irritable, and she seemed constantly restless. He even saw her smoking kissweed with some others, even though she'd been vocal about the stupidity of it.

They spoke from time to time, but he began to wonder whether she even listened to him. But she didn't speak much, so he did most of the talking, anyway. He tried asking about what had happened—he knew it must have been something—but she just changed the subject. It was the usual "You'll see" and "Just wait, it will be your turn soon enough" answers, which irked Dave something fierce. He had begun to hate those words. He wanted to know. If it was bad, he'd handle it. He even said as much, and Liz just laughed.

"If I could tell you, I might. But I can't." And that was the end of it.

After a few weeks, Liz came over and told him she would be gone for a long time, something to do with the Rift. He just nodded quietly, understanding he'd get no answers to any of his questions. Instead, he buried himself in his own specialization. For a few more weeks, he managed to fool himself that if he buried himself deep enough in electronics, computers, and advanced technology, the alarm would never wake him again, he wouldn't have to go out and face whatever it was that Liz had seen. Maybe he wouldn't be… changed, like she was.

SUE

The ceremony was impressive. There were no other words to describe it. For a week, the Janissaries of Camp Sharpe had been busily preparing, setting up a great stage, creating a show of fireworks and laser effects, advanced stage lighting, sound effects, music, and a huge screen in the background. There were flowers, banners, and Covenant flags everywhere. Everyone knew their place and everything had been rehearsed over and over again. The honor guard surrounded the stage, all along the walk up to it, and all the way back to the airpad. The cameras were everywhere, while behind the scenes, electronic defense systems would prevent any unexpected interference, and every armed man and woman not attending the ceremony was manning positions covering every entrance. Above, the airships, brandishing all kinds of weapons from machine cannons to rockets to laser defense systems, patrolled the air.

Sue thought it was all too much, but it was out of her hands. She had done what she thought was best, and somehow the story had reached all the way back to Legacy. When she had spoken to Counselor Novak, she'd had no idea it would lead to this. Nevertheless, she didn't see how she could have done anything differently. It had never been up to her, anyway.

Head Servant Lunde stood before her, beaming. She avoided his eyes. The medal he held up before her looked heavy. It was white gold, brandishing the Covenant symbol in black. The Exceptional Deed of Bravery Medal. It had only been awarded to Janissaries four times before, and never to one still considered an initiate. Granted, she was no longer an initiate, but she had been when she did what had led to her nomination.

"...And here you have her," the head servant said to the camera in front of them. "Susan Atlas." Everyone cheered, and the screen showed the flapping flag of the Covenant morphed with her face. The music, a patriotic hymn everyone knew, was loud. The head servant's words were louder still.

"A young woman, saving her friends and exhibiting exceptional bravery under fire. An example for future generations of what Service to the State means." Sue cringed, but kept up appearances. For the previous week, since the announcement, she had been interviewed so many times, she had lost count. She was being portrayed as the young woman from a small town, doing her duty, serving bravely in the most dangerous environment. Nobody mentioned that she hadn't seen combat at all since coming back from the mission where they lost Brad. Nobody mentioned Brad at all. It was all about her, a woman on her way to the responsibility of citizenship, an example for every young man and woman out there.

The cameras broadcast everything into mandatory viewings in every home in the Covenant. She should have been thinking of her mother and Jason. Of her father, who would have been so proud to see her like this. So relieved that his daughter would have a different life than he'd had. A longer life even.

But all she could think of was the young woman she had killed. The one she had taken prisoner, and then shot as the woman pulled a hidden gun on her. That wasn't bravery; it was sloppiness.

She looked at the audience and saw at least one man who didn't think of her as a hero. First Janissary Ivanov had come, and he was fuming. She realized she had deeply offended him when she stood up for Dave on Initiation Day, and he didn't seem like the type to forget easily. It was a wonder really, that he hadn't stopped the whole thing, but she guessed that spoke volumes of the influence of Counselor Novak. This was his doing, although Head Servant Lunde seemed to enjoy the occasion immensely.

She saw Tac Hordvik standing to attention just below the stage, beaming like a proud big brother. Sub Strategos Janev looked equally proud, standing just as stiffly beside the tacticus. As if this was his doing somehow. Her eyes darted around, finding her team. There was Keisha, brandishing a big grin, ear to ear, winking as their eyes met. Quinn, surprisingly cheerful and finally out of hospital. She thought she sensed a certain respect. That was unexpected. Julian stood there, as well, smiling at her. She looked away. Ever since they got back, there had been a tension between them. And it wasn't uncomfortable. She felt her cheeks go hot and tried to think of something else, turning her attention to the head servant, who looked like he was ready to finish.

"Thank you, thank you all," he said and turned toward her.

"But most of all, Sub Tacticus Atlas, thank you." He extended his hand, and her alarm seemed to amuse him greatly. Sub Tacticus? She had been an initiate just a few weeks ago. It was unheard of. She took his hand and shook it, head spinning. Then Head Servant Lunde took off her single Junior Janissary bar from her lapel and pinned the triple bar of her new rank in its place. He turned, gave a big smile to the camera, and waved all around, making sure the camera got it from every angle, before walking off, followed by his aides and security detail from Legacy.

Sue watched his back as he disappeared. As the cameras were switched off, people rushed in to greet her.

"Congratulations, Sub Tacticus," Tac Hordvik said, shaking her hand.

Keisha slapped her back.

"You're famous now, girl," she said. "You're a heroine! A few more years, and you'll be government material. I'm telling you, you're set for life now. And a long life!" Sue smiled, relieved that this was finally over. Back in Legacy, and in every town all over the Covenant, people would watch the broadcast and the reruns, over and over. But here, tomorrow was a new day. This would all blow over, and people would forget about all of this. She would be a bit young for a SubTac, but that would be it. Soon, everything would be back to normal.

Chapter 8

SUE

The next day, while Tac Hordvik led them through contact drills, fine-tuning their moves, making them act like a single organism, Sub Meridian Hoston came over. He stood there for a moment, watching them practice, before he waved them over. They lined up beside the tacticus.

"Tacticus Hordvik, it is time for the transfer." Hordvik straightened, and the sub meridian continued to read their new placements from an infopad. Sue was to go to the Westfold Brigade with Julian and Keisha, while Quinn was being sent east to the coast, to join the Kosmopol Brigade.

They ended practice at lunchtime, and after eating, Sue went to pack her belongings. She was happy about the outcome. She got to stay with her friends, and although she got along well enough with Quinn these days, she wouldn't consider him a friend. She would miss the tacticus, though. After getting to know him better, and having listened to him at Survivor Night, she had grown to respect him even more.

When she entered the barracks, she started. Tac Hordvik stood by her bunk, waiting.

"Susan," he said, and she walked in. She didn't know what to say, so she just waited for him to speak.

"The Westfold Brigade is a good unit. And you will do well there," he said.

"Sure," she said. She had no idea whether the Westfold Brigade was a good unit or not. "Actually, I'm not even sure where it is, Westfold."

He smiled.

"Westfold is the westernmost part of the northern borderlands of the Covenant. In fact, if you go south from Westfold, you will reach Warden territory. As far as I know, our people don't have much to do with them, though, even out in Westfold. But I'm sure I don't know half of what happens out there," he said. Then he looked at his watch.

"I have to go now. Counselor Novak made me realize something about myself, and I have accepted a placement with the Strategos Command back in Legacy. I might be back later, though, if it gets too boring." Sue smiled back at him and realized this might be the last time she saw him. Tac Hordvik had taught her everything she knew, and now they were both going in their separate directions. She straightened and slammed her fist to her chest.

"It's been an honor, sir," she said. He did the same, a bit more slowly, before he spoke.

"The honor is all mine, Atlas." Then he smiled again before he turned and walked away.

Sue didn't waste much time packing. She didn't have

much to pack, anyway.

Five minutes later, she was on her way to the train platform with Julian and Keisha. It was strange, the last time she had gone by train had been with a friend, as well, but this time there was none of the uncertainty. Sure, she felt the excitement and wondered how her new unit would be, what kind of commander she would get, and what sort of tasks she would be assigned. And there was always the uncertainty of knowing that, at any time, she could be sent on a mission that ended badly. Janissary casualty rates were known to be high; that's why nobody expected Janissaries to serve beyond their mandatory three years. But she had done well at Camp Sharpe, and she had been in combat, where she had done even better. She still felt a pang of regret thinking of the woman she had shot, but everyone kept telling her she wasn't to blame and that there was nothing she could have done differently. So she tried not to think too much about it.

The train ride was much faster than the last time, too. The maglev lines going from east to west were designed to carry troops and supplies quickly to wherever they were needed. So after two hours, the train came to a stop, and everyone got off, stepping out onto the platform.

"Over here, Janissaries," a tacticus shouted from behind the platform proper. They walked over. Sue wondered whether to come to attention or salute. Regulation said they should, but there was something about the woman, a casual style and a somewhat relaxed smile, that made her hesitate. Julian did, though, and the tacticus laughed.

"Yeah, yeah," she said, "you can quit that now. This ain't Camp Sharpe. Here we do things a bit differently." Sue cocked her head, noticing the smell. Sweet. She had another look at the woman, and noticed the look on her face. It wasn't just her being relaxed or a more laid back attitude around camp. Her pupils were slightly dilated, and she had a dumb smile on her face. She was affected by something, Sue realized.

"So welcome to Camp Gustavson. Let's get you bunked up, shall we?" the tacticus said. "Follow me."

The three of them followed the woman to a building toward the center of camp. Inside, she noticed the No Smoking signs.

"See that?" the tacticus said. "No smoking." She giggled.

"So keep it outside, all right? And if you need anything, and I mean anything, I'm right over there, in Supply. Just ask for Anna." She pointed at a nearby building, where a bunch of crates were being carried inside by a group of Janissaries.

"All right then..." she continued, looking down at her infopad, searching with her finger until she found what she was looking for.

"We go by first names here, okay?" She looked down again.

"Keisha and Julian, you are housed in here. Just grab a free bunk; there should be plenty. Most of the guys in this room got caught up in an ambush last week. Those who made it won't be coming back here, so just make yourselves at home." Sue saw the stunned looks on her friends' faces before they went inside. Anna didn't wait for them and continued walking. They reached a room at the back of the building and went inside.

A lean fellow got up from his chair and extended his hand.

"Rory Sanders," he said. Sue took his hand and shook it.

"Susan Atlas," she said.

Although not very muscular, he looked wiry and strong, with a firm jaw and a mustache that made him similar to Tac Hordvik, in an odd way. From his looks, she could have sworn he was Moon people, but the name gave him up as just a regular guy from some small town, like her.

"So, I trust you'll take good care of her, Rory. Let her know what's what and who's who." The tacticus turned to Sue.

"And don't let him be too strict. He's a third-year vet,

but you still outrank him. If you wanna come smoke, you do that, no matter what he tells you. You may need it, even if he don't." Sue nodded at her before Anna turned and walked away.

Rory motioned toward one of the bunks.

"Get yourself situated, Sub Tacticus. The rest of the guys are having dinner, so they'll be back in about an hour." Sue walked over and put her pack on a bunk that seemed unoccupied. She noticed Rory watching her, and turned toward him.

"So when do I meet my unit? Is this it? This room, I mean." He nodded.

"We don't usually get the green ones," he said, looking her up and down. "Green as grass, but already a sub tacticus. And assigned here, to the QRF. You must be special." He looked honestly surprised, now that Sue noticed. So he hadn't seen the show then, thankfully.

"QRF?" she asked. Rory smiled.

"Quick Reaction Force. If something happens, we're the first to go. And something does happen around here." He motioned toward the door.

"The Westfold Brigade is a pretty good unit, and we see our share of action. You might have got the wrong impression, though, from her. It's the kissweed from down south that messes people up. Look at Anna, Moon blood and all. She could have had anything. Instead, she chooses to stay, doing a shit job, high more often than not. Probably disowned by her family, I mean, she's been her for as long as anyone can remember. But for some reason, the officers never crack down on it. Seems they think it's all right for some reason. Shit." He shook his head, but didn't say anything more.

Sue hadn't seen anything like kissweed at Camp Sharpe, but then again, that was a training unit. These guys saw combat all the time. She could figure some of them needed to unwind, although she wondered if there wasn't a better way than by smoking kissweed. She changed the subject.

"So I'm supposed to be part of this QRF then. Is there some kind of training or something I have to go through first?" Rory grinned.

"Sure. As soon as we can get you suited up and get us a mission, we'll go out there and train. And you'd better learn, Sub Tacticus. Else you die." Sue nodded slowly. She had figured as much, but she had to ask.

"Ever wondered why we Janissaries got the highest casualty rates?" Rory asked. "We have a pretty straightforward selection routine, that's what it is. You get through Camp Sharpe, you get thrown into the water. Sink or swim, live or die. A lot of people die." He leaned back, rocking back and forth on two of the chair's legs.

"You're lucky, though. The QRF got the toughest assignments, but we're also the best unit in camp. And that's not just something I'm saying. If you're going swimming in the deep waters, having competent people around you can make all the difference. We're pretty serious, you'll see. And none of us smoke, either." Sue finally smiled. She found she liked the man.

"Sounds good," she said. "Just one thing, and let me assure you, this is just because I'm curious, not because I'm planning to be the first smoker in the QRF. That kissweed, you said it comes from the South. You mean Covenant south? I'm from the South, Charlestown, and I've just barely heard of it. Or did you mean Corpus lands?" Rory shook his head.

"No, no, not that far. I meant Warden territory. They bring in supplies all the time, Weapons, ammo, high tech gadgets of every kind. Kissweed. Other stuff." Sue raised her eyebrows. She had no idea. She thought of Dave, from back home, who had gone to the Wardens after she talked his way out of being sent to the Corpus. What on Earth was going on down there?

DAVE

Dave was deep in thought when the alarm sounded. He'd been trying to solve a particularly difficult problem in which an algorithm meant to fool a secure folder into thinking he had pressed a correct password code didn't perform as expected. Instead, it made the folder initiate a self-destruct sequence, which was about as far from what he wanted as he could get. He cursed silently. Having lost his concentration due to the alarm, he logged off the training interface, grabbed his jacket, and walked out. The sunlight blinded him for a moment, and he squinted. He was expecting this to be like the last time the alarm sounded and was surprised when nobody stood by the door to hand out weapons and ammo. He kept walking until he reached the square, where everyone was gathered. A Moon blood Warden he knew as Kirilov was calling out names.

"Greer, Baldwin, Scott, Wagner." Dave was certain he'd heard wrong, but Kirilov repeated the names until everyone was gathered around him.

"Let's get you suited up and fit for fight. Follow me," he said.

The four initiates walked after Kirilov, who stomped briskly over toward the building near the airpad, where he'd seen Liz go when she returned from her first patrol. Kirilov ushered them inside.

The inside of the building looked nothing like he'd expected. The outside had the markings of a hospital, but this looked more like something of a cross between a lab and a warehouse. There were people he'd never seen before, in white coats. They looked like doctors. Or lab technicians. No way to tell the difference, since Dave had only been inside a hospital once, as a kid, when he'd contracted a particularly nasty strain of flu.

"Get moving; we don't have all day," Kirilov said. A female doctor led them down a long hallway until they reached a door at the end. She opened it and motioned without a word for them to enter. Inside, a young man with distinct Moon people features stood preparing four syringes. The medical assistant turned, and Dave noticed the blood shot eyes and stubble on his cheek.

"Juri, thank you," the woman said. "You can take the rest of the day off." He mumbled an incomprehensible reply and left the room. The doctor spread her hand apologetically.

"He's been up for forty-eight hours straight, working," she said. Dave shrugged it off. Poor sod.

The woman, Thorvaldsen, according to her name tag, motioned for him to sit, and he took a seat as she picked up one of the syringes.

"Tilt your head," she said. He complied, and she

stuck the syringe into his neck with a steady hand. It hurt like hell, but only for a second, before the anesthetic numbed his skin. He'd had his share of shots in school, but only a couple of times had he gotten this kind of syringe. The difference was huge. This way, he didn't feel a thing when she pressed the contents into his bloodstream.

"What is it, vaccine?" he asked. The woman just smiled, while Kirilov sneered.

"Did someone tell you to speak, Wagner?" he said. Dave didn't reply, and Kirilov let it slide.

"All right, you're all set. You can continue through that door," Thorvaldsen said, still smiling, and Dave got up. As he opened the door to leave, he saw Scott get ready for his shot. The room he entered was empty, with just a table and six chairs. He sat down and touched his neck tentatively. The anesthetic was already wearing off, and it felt sore. He sat back and stared up at the ceiling, where a remote-controlled camera hung, watching him. He leaned to his right. The camera followed. Then he leaned to his left. The camera buzzed and followed him again. Then he got up and moved to the other side of the room. The camera followed. He grinned at it. He wasn't looking forward to whatever was coming, but damned if he'd show it.

A noise from behind a door on the opposite side of the room got his attention. A commotion, feet shuffling, something getting knocked over. Someone was fighting. He walked over to the door, acutely aware of the camera following his every movement. He grabbed the handle cautiously. What could they do, really? It wasn't as if he did something wrong. He opened the door, just a little. Enough to peer through the crack.

Three Wardens were holding someone down, pushing him against the floor, as a doctor holding a syringe struggled to inject the man, careful not to hit the Wardens. Dave watched, stunned, as the poor man got his head twisted so that the doctor could insert the syringe, and then he saw his face. It was Juri. Their eyes met. Juri's eyes were wide open, and when he saw Dave he screamed.

"Ignorance is bliss! Bliss is ignorance! Don't believe..." The tranquilizer worked astonishingly fast, and his eyes glazed over as his head slumped.

Dave shut the door as quietly as he could and took a step back. What the hell just happened?

He knew he shouldn't have seen that. Had they noticed him?

He looked up at the camera again, realizing he'd been watched the whole time. He half expected someone to burst through the doors at any minute, to take him away, lock him up, or whatever they did to people who were too curious for their own good.

The door creaked.

He jumped.

Scott walked in, grinning.

"Shit man, you ready for this? Think we'll get to actually see the Rift this…" he stopped, and Dave realized his face must have given him away.

"What's wrong man?" Scott asked. Dave just shook his head, forcing a smile.

"Nothing, just… I guess it must be the syringe. I hate needles," he said. Scott shrugged and continued talking, but Dave couldn't get his mind off Juri's face. Those eyes had seen something. And whatever it was, it had driven him mad.

SUE

Sue began to familiarize herself with everything and everyone, especially her new teammates, who mostly appeared reluctant to get to know new people. She understood. With the casualty rates of active Janissary units, it was to be expected that people would hold back. Nevertheless, she memorized their names: Rory, Henry, Christine, Alexandra, Raymond, Mikhail, and Oystein. Three Moon people and five English, including herself.

Although her rank warranted team command, her lack of experience meant she wouldn't command anyone for a while yet, which suited her just fine. She never wanted command. But she noticed they all looked at her sideways, wondering. And perhaps there was a little envy, as well, although nobody showed it openly.

She didn't care. She would prove herself soon enough. She hoped.

Rory was the exception to the rule, and she became friends with him from day one. He had a dark sense of humor, which she shared, but he had a serious side, as well, which showed whenever they were rehearsing tactics or cleaning weapons or talking about what lay beyond the border.

"Some of them speak English," he said once. She had been surprised. The only one she had met—the woman she'd killed—had spoken a garbled tongue she didn't understand. She shuddered at the memory.

"Most of them don't, but I know it's true. I heard it myself, once." He continued by telling her about a day almost two years ago, when the northerners had attacked. They had almost overrun the camp, before the Janissaries regrouped, and struck back with everything they had. By the time the airships arrived, there were only scattered enemy pockets left. Rory had been there when one of those pockets surrendered. That was when he had heard one of them speak heavily accented English.

"Where had he learned our language?" Sue asked.

"We'll never know," Rory said. "We executed them all. Orders."

Sue thought about that story as she walked through camp on her way back from the shooting range. Strange to think that these people, the enemy, might be able to communicate with someone from the Covenant, if they could stop trying to kill each other off every time they encountered one another. But she had learned—in school, in basic, and from experience—that the northerners would kill every one of them, if they ever got the chance. The Janissaries were the only thing that stood between civilization and mass murder.

She passed Supply on her way, and Anna stuck her head out, grinning.

"Ah, Susan! You look like you're getting settled in." Sue smiled back. She liked the tacticus. Didn't understand her—who understood Moon people, except the Moon people themselves—but liked her, definitely. Anna was an outcast, from what Rory had told her, but here, among brothers and sisters of arms, she had found her new home. There was a sadness about her, masked by a cheerful face and kissweed, but she seemed content with her life, somehow.

"Are Rory and the others treating you well?" Anna asked. Sue nodded, smiling back at her.

"Yes, Tacticus. Everything's fine," she replied. Of

course, she didn't have any new friends yet, and she didn't see much of Keisha and Julian. Some of the QRF people might become friends, given time, but not yet.

"Good, good... And if you ever need anything, you know where to find me," Anna said, as she usually did. Sue didn't say anything as Anna's head disappeared inside again.

She heard the whine a moment before Supply exploded.

One moment there was quiet, a nice and sunny winter day, with just a few wisps of snow in the air. The next, it was as if she had stepped into the fires of hell. Supply was a wreck, with everyone inside dead or dying. Anna...

More whines filled the air, and impacts turned the camp into a scene of random carnage. Buildings exploded and burned; the wounded lay screaming; and the dead littered the ground all around. Sue stood as if frozen, noticing the sounds had become muffled. It must have been one of the first blasts. What now? What to do?

"Hey, Atlas! Atlas!" Rory's voice. She looked around. Rory was peeking out from behind a corner, waving his hand at her.

"Sue! What are you doing?"

She realized she was standing up, in the middle of the street, while everyone else still able to walk had taken cover. She ran over to where Rory was standing. She clutched her rifle tightly, knuckles white. Rory grabbed a hold of her as she rounded the corner, pushing her toward the wall.

"Concrete," he said. "Better than nothing." He looked around the corner again. Sue noticed the rest of the QRF were there with Rory. Raymond was holding a rocket launcher, but except for him, they were carrying only light weapons, rifles mostly.

"Shit, we aren't prepared for this. Too many green initiates."

"I'm not an initiate anym…" Sue protested, but he ignored her. She held her breath.

"We need to get to the barracks," he said. He looked at her.

"How many rounds you got left, Sue?" She looked at him inquisitively, and he continued.

"Never mind, it's not enough, anyhow. Like I said, we need to get to the barracks. Got everything we need over there."

Christine was leaning around the corner now.

"It's still standing," she said. That meant Keisha and Julian would be alive, if they were inside. Sue felt a pang of regret for not being with them now.

"All right then," Rory said, "two lines, we move quickly. This is artillery—and I cannot for the life of me understand how those savages have got their hands on such weapons—but it means they can't see us. So let's just move as fast as we can. Don't worry about cover." They all nodded, gritting teeth, setting their jaws, bracing for what's next.

"Now!" Rory shouted and jumped out into the carnage. Everyone followed, and Sue tried not to step on the wounded as they ran among the dead and the dying. Ten seconds, fifteen, twenty. She sprinted with everything she had, and her lungs already cried for air. Thirty, thirty-five. Habit made her count the seconds, although it didn't matter at all. She would keep running until she reached the barracks. It seemed an eternity, every second possibly her last.

And then she slammed against the door, first one to reach the barracks, with Rory a split second behind. He grabbed the door handle and flung the door open.

"Inside, quick!" he said. As they ran through the hallways, Rory spoke into a handheld device. She didn't hear him over all the commotion. Through every door, she saw people donning Janissary suits, loading weapons, getting ready.

"Sue! You're all right!" she heard a familiar voice call out. She turned toward the sound. It was Julian, and he smiled warmly at her. Sue almost choked up as she threw an arm around his neck, hugging him. She saw Keisha out the corner of her eye, zipping up her suit and checking her helmet before she lowered her visor.

"Atlas, get moving! No time for lover boy, we've got work to do," Rory shouted, and she let Julian go. She turned around without a word and followed Rory into the QRF quarters. She sat down on her bunk, packing her escape pack on top of the larger long-range pack, the way they usually packed for long-range patrols.

"Leave the LR; we need to move quickly. Just the EP this time," Rory said. She nodded and put the EP on her back, outside of her weapon straps and tac vest.

"You know, Julian and me, we're just friends…" Sue said, and Rory stopped dead, eyes cold.

"Sub Tacticus Atlas. Do I really look like I care?" He paused, then turned away.

"Just get ready. We move out in thirty seconds."

Sue had time to check the distance settings on her sights one last time. A brief pat down to make sure all of her ammo pouches were secured, and a quick swig of water from the sink, never touching her full canteen.

"All right, guys," Rory said loud enough for everyone to hear. The sounds of destruction were muted by walls and windows, but Sue was glad he almost shouted, since her hearing still hadn't fully returned from the first blasts. Rory stood broad legged in front of them. She was glad he took charge. Even if he didn't outrank anyone, he held a natural authority, and everyone followed his lead.

"Listen up. Brigade Command has located the enemy artillery, but it's too mobile and too close for them to strike back, unless they want to take out the entire camp here. So we do it. We go in hard, fast, and without mercy. That means no prisoners." Sue heard someone muttering behind her. Rory cut it off.

"Yes, I'd love to take prisoners, too. We could learn a lot from that. But right now, our mission is to destroy that artillery. That's it. Got it?" He spoke into his handheld again.

"This is the QRF, moving out."

Chapter 9

SUE

The Quick Reaction Force ran first toward the outpost closest to where the artillery had been located. The tacticus in charge there seemed relieved to meet Sue and her team, and as the four-man team blasted away into the forest beyond the perimeter, Rory received directions to a path that would take the QRF around and to the west of the enemy position. They wasted no more time, and snuck out to the left, leaving the outpost to continue firing at the unknown enemy.

"Won't they ever run out of ammo?" Sue asked. Oystein, one of the Moon people from her team, grinned while clutching his own weapon.

"Sure they will. In about two days, if they keep firing like that." He laughed at her surprise. "They have a stash beneath the outpost, loaded with ammo, spare weapons, food, you name it. Trust me, Susan, nobody gets past that, even if there are only five of them."

"So even if they're not replenished, they can hold out, firing like crazy, for two days?" she asked. Oystein nodded.

"That's right. And there are outposts like that all along the perimeter. The Westfold Brigade will stand its ground, don't worry."

They moved in silence once they passed the minefields north of the outposts. It wasn't far, but they moved carefully, since they were now officially inside enemy territory. Reaching the artillery position took them almost half an hour, and by the time the arrived, the enemy force had moved on.

"Shit," someone in the back mumbled. Rory and Christine were studying the ground on the far side of the position, and after a moment, they gathered everyone.

"They moved out of here just minutes ago. We can follow them or we can wait for them to get away. Either way, the attack on camp is over, so our main task is completed," Rory said.

"Fuck that," Oystein spat. "They'll just come back. I say let's get them while they're close. We won't have an opportunity like this for a while."

"There might be more of them," Raymond said.

"We're better than they are, and we have better equipment. I say we crush them now," Alexandra said. If Sue didn't know better, she'd believed she was Moon blood, as well, the way she spoke. She had a bad feeling about this, but being the fresh face around, she kept quiet.

"All right, we do it," Rory said, determination apparent on his face. "Attack formation, half speed, fire at will." They would overtake the enemy shortly, even at half speed, since the QRF was lightly equipped, whereas the enemy would be carrying a heavy load. They had found no tracks, which meant they were carrying the artillery. Everyone spread out, and soon they were moving through the woods.

"Stay sharp. I want the first shot fired to be ours," Rory's voice whispered inside her helmet. He didn't have to ask Sue twice. She knew she was walking into combat, and though she hadn't really had time to be afraid the last time out, she did now. She could feel the adrenaline rushing through her veins, and her hands were shaking. She saw enemies in every shadow, and if it hadn't been for the lessons taught by Tac Hordvik, she'd already been firing away, blasting those trees and bushes into oblivion. Scaring away whoever lay out there, she hoped. She wished the suit would inject something to help her calm her nerves, but it had a mind of its own. She had to stay sharp, and though the suit had all kinds of aids available, its main concern was her fighting ability. She had to remain alert, even if it meant clattering teeth, shaking hands, and vision that tricked her into seeing things that weren't there.

It was Christine who fired the first shot, but not at the enemy. The Janissary suits would alert them to explosives hidden in booby traps, but the one Christine stepped into was nothing but a hole, one square meter, hidden by foliage and thin branches. Her scream as she landed on the sharpened stakes pierced Sue's ears even as the suit muffled the sound inside her helmet. Christine's shots went all over, and it was a miracle nobody was hit.

"Trap!" Rory shouted. "On me, baseline front."

Everyone rushed into position, but it was too late. Oystein and Alexandra both fell from the first rounds as enemy fire rained upon them. Sue still had no visual on the enemy. Nothing to fire at. She kept her rifle ready.

"Get back here!" she heard Raymond scream. Somebody was running. To help someone, to chase an enemy, to get away from it all? No way to tell.

A kick in her chest followed by another, and then a stabbing pain piercing her shoulder. Two shots, deflected by her suit, and one penetrating her armor. She felt the local anesthetic as the nano bots went into action, stitching her up, minimizing blood loss. She realized she was on the ground, surprised at not having noticed her fall. Something moved by in her peripheral vision. Friend or foe? Probably friend, since the suit hadn't done anything. She knew it had a dozen ways to kill anyone who got too close to her while she lay wounded.

Then all sounds inside her helmet went dead, and a red triangle appeared in front of her eyes. Malfunction, low battery. *How can that be? I charged it just yesterday—it should last for weeks*! she thought. Then she rolled over and saw the leak, the tiny darts that had pierced the battery compartment just below her neck. And she saw two others being dragged along, held at gunpoint, all suit defenses incapacitated.

This was not some random attack, from which the enemy had fled now that the Janissaries were counterattacking. They had been lured out here, so the enemy could capture at least some of them alive. Sue suddenly realized that the northern savages, the primitive people who were a major nuisance but never considered a real threat, had just outmaneuvered the Janissaries, captured a closely guarded technology, and were now holding Sue and probably more of her teammates captive.

DAVE

The airship ride was dizzying and confusing. It wasn't so much the ride per se. Dave had never been up in the air before, but the ship was big and the seats comfortable. It was the drugs running through his veins that were beginning to affect his vision and his sense of balance.

"I thought it was just a vaccine," he said to Scott, who sat right next to him. Scott looked like he was about to throw up and didn't reply. Kirilov though, grinned at him.

"It is," he said. He didn't look like he was affected at

all, unlike Greer, who looked just as bad as Scott. As bad as Dave felt. He looked over at Baldwin, who sat with his eyes closed. That seemed to work better, so he closed his eyes, as well, until they popped open two seconds later. Didn't work at all, at least not for him.

"We are going to intercept a group of infected. If they get past the zone, they will spread all kinds of disease. The vaccine will protect you, though. As will these." Kirilov nodded toward the weapons crate secured between them.

"How do we know they are infected? What kind of infection is it, anyway?" Dave asked. Kirilov looked amused by the question.

"You'll know. It will take you but seconds, trust me."

Scott suddenly grabbed at his emergency airsickness bag and managed to throw up in it, instead of all over himself.

"Yuk!" Greer said, but Dave could see he was struggling not to do the exact same thing. Scott heaved, still holding the bag in front of his face.

"This is so bad," he said, voice muffled. Dave exhaled, trying to think of something else. But thinking was growing increasingly difficult. His mind was all jumbled, and he couldn't focus on a single thought no matter how hard he tried. He even missed the descent, so when the airship's anchor hit the ground, making the ship rock a little, he was unprepared. The senior Wardens, all Moon blood, laughed at the rookies. Greer couldn't hold it anymore and threw up in his bag, and even Baldwin, who had managed to hold it together for so long, stumbled as he tried to get to his feet.

"Everyone, be very careful. We disembark in thirty seconds," Kirilov shouted, so that everyone stopped and paid attention. He produced night vision goggles, one pair each, and handed them out.

"Put the goggles on and press the switch on the right. They will adjust to your vision." Dave put his on, fastened them to the helmet, and pushed the switch. It felt a bit different from training, but he'd get the hang of it soon enough. As long as you paid attention to where you put your feet, the goggles had a wide visual area, enough that he didn't have to move his head all the time. It felt natural. Then he inserted a small bud into his ear and heard Kirilov's voice clearly. He focused on Kirilov.

"Never, I repeat, never take the goggles off. They are part of your protection. And don't forget, the infected are lethally dangerous and should be treated as such. Don't let any of them get too close. And look after each other." He produced a small canister and took out four red pills.

"Take these. Your sickness is part of your reaction to the vaccine. These will help." Dave took his pill and swallowed it immediately. Kirilov smiled.

"Right, let's move out," he said and stepped into the cage, taking Baldwin and Scott with him. The fourth man inside was one of the Moon blood seniors. Dave didn't know his name.

The first team descended quickly, and then it was Dave's turn. Kirilov had returned with the cage and commanded them all on board. Dave went first. Greer came after, still struggling with the straps of his goggles and trying not to stumble as he entered the cage. Another nameless Moon blood senior was last on board.

The cage descended so quickly, Dave thought they were going to crash. But in the last instant, the speed decreased, and they landed smoothly on the ground.

"Out, quickly," Kirilov commanded. His voice, barely a whisper, was still loud enough to hear clearly, because of the ear bud. Dave lifted his rifle, searching through the optical scope for movement. He saw that Scott held something that resembled a machine gun, and one of the seniors was assisting him. Kirilov held some sort of mini assault rifle, and the rest had ordinary rifles like Dave. He looked up and saw the airship was gone. Only then did he notice how silent it must have been.

"Light and sound discipline in effect," Kirilov said quietly. "They are less than one k away, to the northwest. We move to that tree line and set up an ambush." Dave concentrated on the words and found he had no problem understanding and processing them. He could think again. And his vision and balance were beginning to feel better, as well. In his peripheral vision he noticed little flickers, but he figured it had to be the lighting optimizer working to make use of every light source available.

Then he felt—more than he heard—movement behind him, buzzing by.

"What..." he whispered, before Kirilov turned toward him, a hard look in his eyes.

"That's the observation drone, you idiot. Now quiet," he said. Dave flushed. Of course. The drone would be filming them, recording everything. This was not just a rite of passage; it was also a test. If someone didn't pass, they might end up in the Corpus. Or so he'd heard.

They moved swiftly, but quietly, and within a few minutes, they had reached the spot where they would set up the ambush. They were hidden a few meters inside the thick woods, with a clearing in front of them and an area of scattered brush on the far side, about two hundred meters away.

"Scott, in the middle here. Greer, left flank. Baldwin, right flank. Wagner, between Scott and Greer." Kirilov directed them into position. Dave felt light headed, a mix of fear and euphoria. He almost didn't notice that the seniors took up positions behind them. Probably so that they could support them whenever needed. He shook off a bout of dizziness and focused on the task at hand. He looked through his scope.

They waited for a few more minutes. The only sound was their breathing and some directions from Kirilov in their ears. Watch your ammo count. Be ready. Look after your teammates.

The brush on the far side of the clearing moved.

"Hold it. Let them come all the way out," Kirilov whispered. Dave felt his palms slick with sweat. He adjusted his grip, never taking his hands from the weapon, though. He closed his left eye and peered through the scope.

The monster that entered the clearing was the most fearsome sight he had ever seen.

Chapter 10

DAVE

"Hold your fire. Wait for my signal," Kirilov's whisper was inaudible except for the ear bud that amplified the sound inside Dave's ear, making the order clear and loud enough. Dave felt a shiver running down his spine, but his finger on the trigger was remarkably steady. He blinked. The flicker in the corner of his vision was a nuisance, and though he mostly managed to ignore it, he was afraid it could hinder his aim. Once they got home, he would have to see if it could be fixed. Hasle might have some ideas.

The monsters moved slowly but steadily toward them, and Dave took aim at one of the larger ones. They looked like a mix of images he'd seen in children's books, ancient beasts conceived to frighten kids. Most walked on their hind legs, while others used all fours. He even noticed one being carried by a larger one. Probably its mother. Even the baby monster looked fearsome, like it could devour a grown man.

He looked over at the others. Scott aiming at the center, Greer at the one on the far left, and Baldwin at the one furthest to the right. Scott would probably cut down half their number with the machine gun within seconds.

"Listen up." Kirilov's low voice inside his ear cut his

thoughts off. "Once we open fire, they will spread out. So cover the flanks while Scott does the heavy lifting. Wagner, you pick off anyone trying to move closer. I don't want any of them getting away, so once we're done, we move out and finish them off up close. Remember, they will kill you if you show the slightest weakness. So be swift and ruthless. And whatever you do, do not remove your goggles." A trickle of sweat reached the corner of Dave's goggle, but he gritted his teeth and tried to ignore the itch. He certainly wouldn't contradict Kirilov's orders.

"Everyone get ready…"

Dave saw one of the monsters stroking the back of a smaller one that seemed to have a hard time keeping up. The small one let out a yelp, and the larger growled in response.

"Fire!"

A deafening sound erupted, yelps and growls forgotten. Scott's machine gun rattled, the bangs indistinguishable from each other. Dave hesitated for a moment, enough for him to lose his aim. Where was that beast he'd been aiming at. From the right flank, a series of bursts kicked in, decimating the monsters on Baldwin's side. Dave still tried to find his aim, but gave up and fired wildly into the flock. The monsters fell, blood spattering all over as they tried to run for cover. But there was no cover to be had, and one after another they fell, writhing, screeching, yelping.

It was slaughter.

"What the hell is this?" The shout from his left made him look up. Greer was half way standing, and Dave saw he had put his weapon down.

"What have you done to us? Why…" Greer screamed hysterically, until his chest erupted, and he fell to the ground, eyes and mouth wide open, goggles pushed up on top of his helmet like a second pair of eyes.

"Sniper!" he heard Kirilov shout, and he took aim again. The monsters were all down now, but he scanned the far side of the clearing, searching for the sniper.

"Damn it, why didn't the rangers pick this up?" one of the seniors asked, before Kirilov cut him off.

"Shut up, Jan. You know the enemy sometimes trails the monsters. Everyone, we have to make sure they are all dead. Let's move it. Seniors watch for the sniper; juniors watch the monsters."

"What about Greer?" Scott said, and Kirilov sneered in response.

"He's dead, and he brought it upon himself. Standing up like that… Now move!" The three remaining junior Wardens stood up, and walked toward the carnage, the seniors following a few steps behind.

"Shit," Baldwin whispered. The silence was palpable, and only their breathing and a soft whisper of branches moving in the slight breeze broke the quiet.

"Remember, keep your goggles on at all times," Kirilov spoke sternly. A movement in his peripheral vision made Dave flinch and half-turn, but it was just the irregular flicker.

"What is it, Wagner?" Kirilov asked.

"Nothing, Sir. Just something interfering with my goggles."

"Hold it, let me see." Kirilov walked up to him and put something, an electronic device Dave had never seen before, up in front of him.

"What do you see?" he asked. Dave hunched his shoulders.

"Nothing, just that box or whatever it is." Kirilov seemed to relax and put the box away in his pocket.

"Good. Now, everyone, let's get this done so we can go home."

SUE

The first thing Sue noticed was the clean sheets. Then it was the white walls and the spotless coveralls on the nurses milling about. She remembered being captured by the northerners, so the cleanliness of this place surprised her. She had been taught the people beyond the border were dirty savages, and even the thought of them having something resembling a hospital was contrary to everything she'd envisioned of these people. For a moment, she believed she had been saved by a Janissary rescue squad and brought back to Camp Gustavson.

But the language spoken around her was neither English nor the strange words that some of the Moon people sometimes spoke among themselves. She instantly recognized the sounds, reminding her of her first time in combat. Of a woman taken prisoner. A woman she had shot.

Sue lifted her head, but a headache forced her down again.

"Careful, mademoiselle. You have lost much blood." A man's voice, in accented English. He bent over her, and she saw a man with features that could have belonged to a pure Moon blood if not for the words that came out of his mouth.

"You need rest, for now. Don't worry… Atlas, is that it? Hmm, English then, am I correct?" Sue nodded carefully, wondering how he could know her name. A nurse came over and checked a machine standing by the bedside. She spoke a few words to the man and then walked off. Sue tried to raise her hand. Chained to the bed.

"We have to be careful. I'm sure you understand. We will talk more later. Now rest," he said and turned his back on her. She coughed and tried to speak.

"Did any…"

The man turned back again.

"Please, mademoiselle. You shouldn't speak."

She strained to get the words out.

"Did anyone else survive?" she whispered. The man's brow furrowed, and he took a step closer.

"I assume you ask of your own people, yes? The Janissaries."

She mouthed a yes, soundlessly.

"Two more made it here. We lost one on the operating table." Sue thought his eyes looked sad. Curious.

"The woman had lost too much blood. The man lives, though. The rest I'm afraid are dead. As are so many of our people," he finished, about to turn away again.

"You know my name," she said. "What is yours?" The man smiled at her.

"You should not worry about that, Mademoiselle Atlas." He turned and walked away. As he stood by the doors, waiting for them to slide open, he turned to her again, seeming reluctant.

"I am only a doctor," he said.

"Your… name…" Sue said, feeling herself sliding back into unconsciousness.

"Dr. Conrad Marsden," the man said, his voice

distant, as he disappeared before her eyes, along with the rest of the world.

DAVE

They began the grueling task of checking to see if any of the monsters were still alive. A shot rang out, and Dave saw Scott standing over one of the largest of the beasts. They kept walking.

A medium-sized monster further away was still alive and trying to drag itself away from them. Dave and one of the seniors hurried over, but when they reached the monster, it rolled over. A small sound, a whine, made Dave pause. He thought there was something behind the beast. Bang. The senior Warden, who should be watching for snipers, finished it off.

"Never hesitate. They can get to you," she said. Dave looked at the monster again as it lay still. It was dead, all right.

But there it was again, a whimper, almost like a cat meowing. The larger one had been covering something. Dave walked around it and pushed with his boot at the dead form. It almost made him sick, although something, like a wall, made his emotions feel more distant than usual. He pushed again, and he saw a small claw sticking out.

"Oh, man," he said. "It's got a baby." Dave took a

step back. The senior cursed and kicked the larger form away.

"Oh crap," the senior Warden said, before he fired a burst at the two forms. The mother and the child. Dave stood speechless, and the flicker inside his goggles intensified. He took another step back.

He was about to rip his goggles off, when Kirilov grabbed his hand hard.

"Don't," the older Warden said. Dave tried to object, but Kirilov cut him off.

"Just don't. Or you will wish you hadn't. Trust me." Something in his voice made Dave comply. A shiver, or was it something Dave imagined?

"Let's move out, Wardens. Time to go home," Kirilov said, and everyone followed, eager to get away from it all. Dave hesitated, before he followed like the others.

Dave wondered why nobody was watching for the sniper, but then again, the senior Wardens seemed to know their way around, so it was probably safe. Snipers probably left as soon as they had fired their deadly shots, anyway. That had to be it.

"Just through the trees, and the airship will come pick us up," Kirilov said. Dave looked forward to getting on the airship. He hoped he would never have to go out like this again. This was ranger business, and he was more convinced than ever that Tech was right for him. If he got a chance, he would find a way to fix the goggles, though.

They passed Greer's body, and Dave was about to stop, when Kirilov slapped his back.

"Care for the living, Wagner. He's dead, and now he will return to the Earth that birthed him." Dave looked at the senior Warden, noticing he had a firm grip on his rifle. Determination. He knew the Moon people had notions about death that they never spoke of. While the English were left to rot, anyone of the Moon blood who fell on the battlefield would be taken back. The rumors said their ashes would be sent back to their home world, from where their people had come. Probably just rumors.

Dave glanced back at Greer once more. He lay so still, and there was almost no blood around the small hole in his back. It was almost as if he was asleep, except for the pool of blood he laid in. Dave walked hesitantly along with the others. Something was off, but he couldn't put his finger to what it was.

He still felt as though his mind worked just fine after his brief disorientation.

It wasn't until he sat safely on the airship, on his way back from the slaughter, that he realized how wrong he had been. The realization made him sweat, as he looked around at the others, aware, for the first time, of how wrong everything was.

Greer's chest had exploded.

The exit wound was in his chest.

He had been shot from behind.

His final words, *What have you done to us?*

He had been shot because of those words.

Chapter 11

SUE

She was feeling better, finally. She couldn't remember much of the past few days, only that she had been sliding in and out of consciousness until she finally remained awake long enough to notice more of the people around her. There were six beds in her room. All empty, save hers and one more. The person in the other bed lay on the far side of the room, covered in bandages, unconscious all the time. Sue remembered the doctor mentioning that a man had survived. She tried asking the nurses about him, but got no reply other than confused looks and gibberish in that strange language. None of them spoke any English, it seemed.

On the third day—it must have been three days—the doctor returned. This time, a woman in camouflage uniform came with him. The two had the same angular features and the same sand-colored hair, but hers was cut shorter. And she had stars on her collar.

"Mademoiselle Atlas, meet Colonel Renee Marsden," he said. The woman remained standing, one step behind the man, Dr. Marsden. Sue cocked her head.

"Your wife?" she said without thinking. The two laughed in reply.

"No, mademoiselle," the woman said, "he's my twin brother. You are very perceptive." Dr. Marsden motioned for one of the nurses to fetch chairs, and they both sat down. The doctor looked at his sister before he spoke.

"So, your friend is still unconscious, I hear. I'm sorry. I am afraid he will not wake again." Sue glanced over at the unmoving form.

"Can't you do anything?" Dr. Marsden shook his head.

"If we had your technology... He has sustained severe damages to the head."

"But what if you got him back? What if you could arrange for a prisoner exchange or something?" What was she thinking? How many times had she heard the orders not to take prisoners?

"The Covenant seldom takes prisoners," the woman said, a hoarseness in her voice. "And even if you did, he would never get the necessary treatment. Rory, that's an English name, yes?" Sue nodded, and swallowed hard. So it was Rory, and he was dying.

"Only Moon people get cryo treatment, unless he already earned his citizenship." Sue looked at Rory's unmoving shape. A second-rate citizen, about to give his life for the Covenant. Even if she could somehow break them free, Rory would die. Simply because he was English.

Expendable.

Dr. Marsden got to his feet.

"I'm sorry about your loss, mademoiselle. But I have other patients to tend to. My sister would like a word with you, though, so I will leave you two together." He walked out, and Sue looked at Renee.

"Time for interrogation, then," Sue said drily. The colonel only smiled. Sue thought it must be a high rank, from the way the nurses looked at her, but then she hadn't even known the northerners had ranks.

"I believe we should talk," Renee said.

DAVE

He felt sick. Someone had shot Greer, murdered him for what he had said: *What have you done to us?*

To us. That was the part Dave couldn't understand, no matter how hard he tried. He could easily understand why someone might react as Greer had to the carnage back there. Given the chance, the monsters would probably have slaughtered them all easily, but he could empathize with Greer feeling bad, sick even, for killing the beasts from a distance, one after the other until all were dead. He had heard of other boys in school, going out bow-hunting with their fathers, and after bragging about it in public, they would admit to feeling a little queasy, no matter how necessary the hunt was for feeding the family. Dave had never had to hunt, but he could easily understand how that might make you feel.

To us. The words wouldn't leave him alone. Greer hadn't been the softest of them, either. Dave knew he had applied to the rangers, although he only made security. But he had seemed tougher than all of them, except Scott perhaps.

Kirilov scooted over, and produced a small pack.

"All right, guys, you've just passed your final initiate test. You're full Wardens now," he said, grinning. He opened the pack and let three small blue pills roll out into his palm.

"One each. Final stage of the vaccine. Makes it last longer." They all got one, and Dave swallowed his with some water from his half-full canteen. Better than taking another shot.

Kirilov went to talk to the pilots, while Dave sat lost in thought. When the senior Warden returned, Dave considered telling him of his ideas. Of how Greer had been murdered. Of his final words. Perhaps Kirilov would understand what they meant.

What was it Greer had said? Dave shook his head, struggling to remember. His head was spinning. He needed to remember the exact words. For some reason, the words were important. Which words? What was happening to him? He blinked once, twice, and looked around. Baldwin was sitting next to him, and Scott sat in front with one of the seniors. Kirilov returned, and Dave was about to speak to him, when he found he didn't know what he wanted to say. He laughed softly at his own stupidity. He turned to tell Greer.

Where was Greer?

He considered getting some sleep, but found he wasn't tired. Actually, he was feeling better than ever. Stronger. More alert. He looked at Kirilov and almost guffawed when he saw that the senior Warden had unusually long teeth. Why hadn't he noticed before? He gazed over at Baldwin. Hadn't he been clean-shaven? Now he had a long, bushy beard. Strange. He looked at Scott and sat up straight. His eyes were glowing red, and his grin exposed a set of sharp fangs.

What the hell is happening here? Dave wondered.

"Easy now, Wagner." He heard Kirilov's voice, a note too gravelly. His vision was quickly fading. Scott was laughing hysterically in the background, and an inhuman shriek came from somewhere far away.

"What is happening to me?" he whispered. Kirilov's reply was a growl, almost incomprehensible.

"You are a Warden now. One of us. Time to let go, Wagner." Kirilov's voice grew more distant, and his final words were so far away, Dave wondered if he had actually spoken, or if it was all in his own head.

"Ignorance is Bliss," the voice said.

SUE

"So you are telling me there's a world out there, with people living their lives, and we are not even allowed to know about it? That people get to live until they die from natural causes? That the Moon people didn't save us at all?" Sue shook her head, dumbfounded, and Renee smiled at her.

"I know it's a lot to process, Atlas. And you are more eager than most. Hah, most of those we capture don't believe any of it, at first. They cling to their beliefs like it's a loved one, even when we show them proof of the opposite." She set the books aside and produced her infopad. While she swiped and moved boxes and images around, Renee continued speaking.

"Most end up crying, whether it is from relief or anger or sadness, or all of those reasons, I don't know. That's when I know they are beginning to understand. And nobody ever wants to return. Not even those of the Moon blood. Can you imagine that?"

Sue stared at the map again.

"I knew there had to be others out there, but they taught us you were primitives, scavengers, savages… That the Covenant was a lone beacon of civilization in the world. And yet, look at this map; the Covenant is so small!"

"Beacon of civilization..." Renee grumbled. "Look at this," she said, pointing at a red dot by the sea, far to the north.

"Here's Hudson, our capital. Built from scratch after the Fall, ninety-nine percent underground to protect the people from air raids from the south. Like most of our cities. The Moon people think they have us subdued, but we have never succumbed to them. One day, we will set your people free, as well. After all, we are the same." There was a silence between them while Sue studied the map. Hudson was about the same distance from the Westfold as Legacy, although north instead of southeast.

"Why do some of you speak English, while others speak... I don't know what your language is called..." Sue trailed off, as Renee began to laugh.

"Don't you see, Atlas? We are also English, at least part English. And French, although you probably have no idea what that means." The officer's laugh died, and she began to explain.

"Before the Fall, your land was ruled by the English, but Latin, French and many other peoples lived there, as well. They were basically equals. Up here, my ancestors were English and French, two peoples that had lived together for ages in this land. Most of the English-dominated areas succumbed to the Fall, and the entire western part of this country became a wasteland, while the French, living in the East, managed to save many of their kind. Some of the English survived, as well, and in the frantic final weeks, a lot of people even fled here from the South—your ancestors—because it was said that this land would be spared. Well, it wasn't, not completely, but it fared better than the lands of the South, what you know as the Covenant. So in a way, it is true that the Moon people saved your people, or what remained of them. But at what cost? They enslaved you! Made themselves your masters while you were weak. Those who wouldn't comply fled north, or ended up in camps. That's where they perfected their techniques for euthanasia, by the way. And my people, still too weak to give them a proper fight, had to stand by and watch what they did to you." She fumed now, while her infopad produced images of war, prison camps, and piles of dead bodies.

"But you did fight," Sue said. Renee stopped, and waited for her to speak.

"You have fought for as long as anyone can remember. That's what we were taught in school. That is true at least, isn't it?" Renee shook her head and closed her eyes.

"No, we didn't. We have never fought, except in self-defense, to defend our villages, our children. Once it became clear that the Covenant was too strong to beat, we dug in. We have always skirmished, prodded your defenses, and raided for information, for technology. But we have never tried to tear down the Covenant, as we should have. Because it would have meant the end of us." Sue could see she was deep in thought. After a moment, Renee looked into her eyes.

"There is only one power that could tear down the Covenant, and sadly, it is not us."

"Who is it?" Sue asked. She felt cheated, and a simmering anger at everything she had been taught, everything she had taken for truth—her entire life a lie.

"Who could set things right?" Renee looked at her, as if considering her next words. In the end, one word was enough.

"Buchanan."

Chapter 12

DAVE

"You shouldn't tinker with that." Dave sat up and removed his hands from the keyboard as Senior Technician Hasle entered. Hasle had gone easy on him for the last week since Dave returned from his stint out in the field. The old man probably knew. Probably been there once. Dave couldn't remember all the details, only that there had been something frightening, something trying to kill them all. Monsters. They had gotten Greer. He vaguely remembered being told in debriefing, but everything else was shrouded in a haze. He had one image of Greer lying face down in a pool of blood. Another image of a senior Warden pushing him aside and shooting at something on the ground. Blurry images of firing his weapon, of a flicker inside his goggles disturbing his vision, of Greer shouting something.

What was he shouting? Dave gave up trying to remember. When he thought of it, he didn't really want to remember. He'd had nightmares three nights in a row now. Nightmares of monsters trying to grab him, clawing at him, before they suddenly morphed into a familiar face. Greer, or Liz, or his mom. "Please," they would say, and he'd wake up, sweating and shivering.

"I'm just trying to see if the firewall can hold against a Trojan hidden inside a secure file. You know, using the secure file to gain access, old style, but with better camouflage for the Trojan," he said. Hasle just laughed.

"Come on, Wagner, you don't think that hasn't been thought of? There's a reason they call it old style, you know." Dave nodded. He'd been less creative lately. Probably the nightmares and lack of sleep. Or the drugs. He knew the vaccine had protected him, but why did it have to make him so groggy?

"I think I need a break," he said. Hasle just smiled, and walked over to his own workstation.

"It gets better. Just give it time," the old man said, and Dave suddenly felt enormous gratitude toward his mentor.

"Thanks," Dave said, and walked out.

Outside, he squinted in the harsh sunlight. He walked over to his favorite spot and sat down. He closed his eyes, feeling the warm rays and the cool breeze, and listened to the chirping of little birds in the trees above. A fly buzzed by, and he raised a hand to swat at it.

He sat up, eyes wide open.

The buzzing.

The drone.

SUE

"Who is Buchanan," Sue asked. It sounded like an English name, but that couldn't be.

"Who, and what," Renee said, and got up from her chair, closing her infopad and taking her empty cup with her.

"I'm sorry, Susan, but you will have to find out for yourself. There's so much you should know, and we have so little time..." She checked her watch. It had a small screen, and a voice suddenly came out of it. Sue couldn't hear the words, though. She strained her neck and recognized the face of Dr. Marsden. Renee closed the screen with a quick swipe, hiding the face of her twin brother.

"They are coming. Took them long enough..." she said, removing her sidearm from its holster. Sue looked at her quizzically.

"I would love to stay," Renee said, "but I'm afraid our time is up, and I'm needed elsewhere." She smiled briefly, extending her right arm.

"Ordered elsewhere, that is. It has been a pleasure to meet you, Susan Atlas. I hope we'll meet again, someday." Sue shook her hand, still too surprised to say anything, and Renee quickly walked out, closing the door behind her.

What was that? Sue thought. She looked over at poor

Rory, who would never wake again, would never learn what she had learned. Who would soon be just one more victim of the lies. Lies that had formed their lives, and the lives of those before them. Centuries built upon lies.

She sat for a while, considering the implications. How her life had turned upside down in just a couple of hours. Renee should have been an enemy, but instead she had shown her that there was a world outside the Covenant, and that nothing was as it seemed. Nothing was as she had been taught. It was too much. What was it Renee had said? *They are coming.* What did she mean?

The realization came slowly to her, and a chill went down her spine.

"No," she whispered, "I'm not ready. Oh please, not yet."

The explosion shook the ground beneath her, and the door burst open."

"Two located. One incapacitated, one possible recovery," the Janissary said. Sue managed to get a good look at him as three others entered the room behind him. No, not Janissaries, although the suits looked similar. The weapons looked wrong. And the helmets were different, too.

"Sub Tacticus Susan Atlas?" the first one asked, and she nodded. He removed his helmet. There was no mistaking the features. Pure Moon blood.

"No," she whispered again, although she didn't think anyone heard, or cared.

"Ingolfson, Igorov, stand by for exfil. Olsen, you know what to do," he said. The one named Olsen walked over to Rory and had a look. Then he shook his head.

"Terminate subject," the leader said, and Olsen raised his gun. One shot to the head, and Rory was dead. Sue heard a scream grow louder and louder until she couldn't remain standing and had to cover her ears with her hands.

"Let's move her out," the leader shouted above the scream. Olsen came over and grabbed something in his breast pocket. Sue never felt the syringe before the substance began to make her feel dizzy. Only then did she realize the scream had come from her.

Olsen leaned over.

"Ignorance is Bliss," he whispered in her ear.

Chapter 13

SUE

She heaved for air as she sat up. The sheets were wet with sweat, and her heart was thumping hard. A dream. A nightmare. She'd had a few of those since being snatched back from captivity. She mostly dreamed of Rory, of strangers speaking to her in a friendly manner, before her head exploded in pain. Sometimes, she could see the faces of her team members from the QRF, all dead now. Julian and Keisha came to see her, and she had hugged them both. She had been so relieved when she heard they were both alive and well. She hadn't seen either of them after that, though, and she had a feeling she wouldn't for a long time. She felt a slight sting that Julian hadn't shown up again, but he was probably too busy. Besides, they were just friends. Nothing more.

She got out of bed and pulled on her bathrobe. Her shoulder was stiff, but the pain was gone. She flexed her arm a little. *They enslaved you.* A woman's voice, faint, like a whisper. That was one of the memories that seemed to haunt her. Once she took the pills the doctors administered to her, though, the voice faded away. She knew it would return, but every day the memory got weaker. The dizzying feeling any time she tried to remember something only got stronger, though. She had no idea what it all meant; it was as if everything was buried just below consciousness, trying to break out into the open but kept tightly behind a barrier that grew stronger every day. She walked over to the water cooler and got herself a drink.

She didn't remember much from her days of captivity, but it didn't seem like the intel officers cared much. All they seemed to care about was that she was all right. It was touching, in a way, but it still made no sense. She answered their questions whenever they came, though, and cooperated as much as she could.

But some thoughts she kept to herself. Like the words that pressed on in the back of her mind. *They enslaved you.* And some details were so blurry, she didn't entirely trust them. Like that of the woman's face, looking so similar to the doctor. As far as she knew, it could be one of the doctors in Camp Gustavson, tending to her after her release. They had both spoken English, so she was probably just confused.

A knock on the door broke her train of thought.

"Come in," she said, tying a belt around her waist to keep her robe in place. A tacticus in a fresh uniform entered. He looked around, and Sue was suddenly aware her drapes were still shut, keeping the light out. She smiled and walked to the control panel. She pushed the button, and the drapes folded up along the sides of the great window. She looked out for a moment and saw it was a sunny day. The view toward the green hills was magnificent, and she found herself staring. She turned back to the tacticus.

"I'm sorry, sir. What can I do for you?" The stone-faced tacticus produced a flat envelope and delivered it to her. She cocked her head, and he didn't wait for her question.

"You are requested in Legacy, Sub Tacticus Atlas. Personal request from Counselor Novak himself." Sue heaved her eyebrows. She opened the envelope, tearing off the seal and accidentally ripping into the letter inside. She took it out and held the torn piece so that she could read it.

Counselor Novak had signed the letter, an order to immediately take the first airlift back to Legacy. There she was to present herself to Strategos Command, where they would find a suitable assignment for her. He ended the letter by congratulating her on her heroic performance, and her new rank.

She upended the envelope and a single iron bar fell into her palm.

The tacticus finally smiled.

"I would help you with that, if you wore your uniform," he said.

"Congratulations, Tacticus Atlas."

MARK

He stood on the high balcony overlooking the atrium of Strategos Command, watching as she entered. The young woman had impressed him the first time they'd met, and he had great hopes for her still. It could go one of three ways. She could do extremely well, if she managed to shed all doubt and trust her superiors. If she would give herself to the Covenant and all its splendors, she could be one of the first not of Moon blood to rise all the way to high command. That would be evolution, and Mark Novak would be happy with such a development. If the Covenant changed from within, nothing could be better.

But he had a hard time believing it would happen that way. There were too many obstacles, too many ways for such a person to meet with an abrupt end. That would leave her a medicated citizen who told stories of glory days past, a wreck of a human being inside a near perfect exterior, a poster girl to set an example for future generations of the English, from every corner of the Covenant.

The third possibility was the one he feared the most, but secretly dreamed of. To finally tear down the injustices, the false truths, and the villainy that kept a nation of murderers and slavers afloat. If she saw through the lies and managed to resist, she might have what it would take to succeed. She would have to be careful, though. A lot of people would go to great lengths to keep the status quo.

Mark chuckled. Time would tell, and either way, he had more cards up his sleeve. The man could make a lot of changes, as well. He wasn't as charismatic as Susan, but he commanded respect, and he had seen through many of the lies already. His greatest obstacle was his heritage, his loyalty to his people. Even though he had done his best to deny it for years, he was still of the Moon blood, and he didn't stand a chance of leading the English if it came to blows.

Perhaps if the two could be brought together...

That had been one of his ideas when he sent the letter, requesting her presence here. Of course, he had other plans, as well, but making sure these two weren't far from each other was part of his scheme.

A sub tacticus was leading her away from the atrium, and he figured he would stay in the background for now. His interest in her might raise suspicions. After all, nobody was above suspicion, when the integrity of the Covenant was at stake.

No, he would see how this played out, keeping his cards close to his chest, and wait for one of the others to make the first move.

He walked back to the lounge chair and sat down. Lately, his joints had begun to give him some grief. But what could you expect? He definitely needed the treatment soon. He chuckled again.

He was the oldest man alive, and he intended to keep it that way.

Chapter 14

SUE

Strategos Command was an impressive building, and especially the great atrium. Flags hung from the balconies, black and white Covenant banners surrounding the great open space, where men and women in every uniform she knew, and quite a few others, milled about. She recognized every Janissary variation, of course, but also a few she had never seen in person, such as the Intelligence operatives and Military Academy staff. The Warden uniforms were familiar to her, but only because she had seen the First Warden at Initiation Day. There were few from the Corpus, as expected, while the Students had a number of scholars assigned here, it seemed.

Other uniforms were completely unfamiliar to her, and it surprised her that there were so many of them. But then she had never seen Moon blood units, except for airmen, and she knew there were entire units, numbering thousands of people, that were comprised entirely from Moon people volunteers.

Everyone she saw, regardless of unit or Service, had one thing in common, though, with hardly any exceptions. They were all Moon blood. Even the few from the Corpus had the distinct features of the Moon people.

She wondered why Counselor Novak had sent for her.

"Just follow me through here," the sub tacticus leading her said. He was young, barely seventeen, but had an air of authority about him, the kind that came from the knowledge that he was born to command. She had seen it so many times now, she didn't pay attention to it anymore. She just followed the youngster, wondering where they'd end up.

"This is the Janissary education office, where all basic and advanced training for Janissaries is planned," he said, opening the door for her. She entered, and saw three officers, from head tacticus to meridian, sat in front of computers, swiping documents and images back and forth.

"You will sit over there," he pointed at the desk in the back of the room. The others will fill you in. Just get yourself familiarized with the tech and get to know your colleagues, and tomorrow you will receive your orders."

Sue took a step toward her desk and turned toward the kid.

"My orders?" she said, wondering what she could possibly contribute with here.

"Your task. A word of your advice," he said, puffing out his chest. Sue almost laughed, waiting for him to dispense wisdom gained from his vast experience, "Just do your job here, whatever it is, and you will be on your way to greatness. I saw you, you know." Sue looked at him quizzically.

"The ceremony. With Head Servant Lunde," he said, extending his hand. She took it.

"It's an honor, Tacticus Atlas," he said, and pivoted before he marched out.

As soon as the door closed, someone guffawed from behind her. She turned around and there was Evan Hordvik, grinning at her.

"Tacticus Atlas. How on Earth did you end up in this place?" he asked. Sue let out a somewhat relieved gasp and walked over to him.

"Evan," she said. He smiled knowingly.

"Finally learned my first name, Susan? Well, you couldn't keep calling me Tac now," he said, his silver star stating the obvious. She smiled back.

"Head Tacticus now. So you finally abandoned that foot soldier-forever thing, did you?"

"Hell no! They had to give me a star for me to work here, but if they try to make me meridian or something, I'd like to see them try," he said, grinning even more broadly. Then he walked with her to her desk, where a computer stood waiting for her command. A blue disc flashed softly on the screen, inviting her to touch it. Sue had never used one of these before. The computers they used back in Charlestown were all but obsolete, and fixed up more than once. This one didn't even have a keyboard. She sat down on the perfectly ergonomic chair, and looked at the screen.

"How am I going to write? I assume they want me to write something," she said. Evan leaned over and pressed a finger to the blue disc. It turned red, but nothing happened.

"See? It's already configured for you. I can't open it," he said. Sue put a finger on the disc, and it expanded, revealing a landscape of icons and groups of images.

"So, here on the right are your communication tools. On the left are shared and personal files. Access to shared files depends on your security level. On top are utilities, such as clock, calendar, notes, and so on, and once you get started, all your active stuff will be down at the bottom. In the center, you will find your current assignments. Don't worry, that one tends to fill up quickly." Sue saw there was only one icon in the middle. Welcome, it said. She assumed that was a good place to start.

"How do I control it?" she asked. Back in Charlestown, they had swipe pads and control sticks in addition to the keyboard.

"Look, try to forget how you did things back home. This system is designed to be intuitive. See an icon you'd like to open, just press it, tap it, or spread your fingers from the middle. You can do it directly on the screen, or just on the desk in front of you. The system will learn your habits. Wanna switch screens while multitasking? Just use your palm, swipe from side to side. Wanna close something? Just bring your fingers together or double tap. Everything is designed so that you figure stuff like that out yourself and find methods that work for you." He looked at her as she tapped the Welcome icon.

"Thanks," she said. "Just one more question." She looked up at him.

"Where is the keyboard?" He laughed.

"All right, just look." He opened her message folder. It had just one item, some kind of standard welcome message. He tapped an icon to produce a new message. A cursor blinked in the recipient field, and he tapped it. A blue light projected a perfectly ordinary keyboard onto her desk, right where a physical keyboard would have been placed.

"Now you can write," he said.

~

The welcome icon produced a tutorial for using the computer and several documents regarding her work in Strategos Command, rules, regulations, work expectations, and so on. There was also a long questionnaire, and she filled it out meticulously. A few seconds after she had completed it, she received a message.

The message was automated, a profile sheet based on

her answers on the questionnaire. She didn't pay attention to it—after all, her answers were only partially honest, so an analysis based on them would be faulty in any case.

She looked around. Evan sat with his face to his screen, working on one thing or another. The other two hadn't even said hello yet. As far as she could tell, they were too preoccupied with their tasks to even register her presence. *Some people might think this was a good job*, she thought. She dreaded the prospect of spending her days in this room, in front of this computer, with people who didn't even speak to her. Why had Counselor Novak wanted her to come? She sighed deeply and turned back to her own screen.

A new task had appeared at the center of her screen. She tapped it, and a map opened up. It showed an area stretching from just west of Camp Gustavson to east of Camp Sharpe. The only town on the map was Fort Winter, Keisha's hometown.

The message below the map read: Please indicate the location of your capture. She was puzzled. Was this her task? She tapped the map once, just north of the small dot indicating Camp Gustavson.

The map disappeared, and an image appeared. It was a woman, who looked vaguely familiar. Below her face was a short résumé.

Colonel (Covenant equivalent: Sub Strategos) Renee Marsden
Wanted for subversive activity, specification restricted
Status: Missing
Last known location: North of Camp Gustavson
Extremely dangerous
Terminate on sight

Sue remembered.

Renee, who had told her of the world, and how the Moon people had enslaved them all.

The image disappeared.

"Please answer the following questions," the instructions said.

Sue waited, a knot forming in her stomach. What was going on?

Do you remember this face?—YES
Did this woman speak to you?—YES
Do you remember anything she told you?—YES
Do you remember everything she told you?—NO
Did she mention the history of the Covenant?—YES
Do you believe she told you the truth?—…

Sue hesitated. She knew she shouldn't answer YES. That would condemn her in an instant. She ought to tap NO, right now. She moved her finger closer to the screen, but still she hesitated. Maybe it was a desire to finally stand up to them. Maybe it was uncertainty—after all, she had no way of knowing. Maybe it was the memories, pushing through a barrier somewhere in the depths of her mind, tearing it down, bringing it all back. Even the memory of how the Covenant soldier had stood over Rory while he lay helpless in bed.

A second-rate citizen, expendable, Renee had said. And while that had felt like a blow, it hadn't shocked her. Not really. She had known.

Terminate subject. Like mandatory euthanasia. Once you're spent, you get terminated. She felt her blood boiling. They had tried to make her forget. To make her a pliable little subject again. Medicate her; take away the memories that had shown her the truth. *Ignorance is Bliss*, the soldier had said as she'd passed out.

She remembered now.

And still she hesitated.

She tapped the NO icon frantically. Too late. She turned away from the screen.

The men who had been sitting in front of their own screens got up. They looked straight at her. Both were holding guns, pointing at her. Evan stood up, as well, looking confused and angry at the same time.

"What the hell is going on?" he said.

"Sit down, Hordvik," one of the men said, moving his weapon slightly.

The door opened, and a man walked in, followed by armed soldiers. She instantly recognized the face. The last time she had seen it, he had been looking straight at her, a threat apparent in those ice blue eyes. She had almost forgotten. He stood in front of her now, all six feet, hovering over her. That same black suit, white close-cropped hair and a face set in stone.

"First Janissary Ivanov," Sue said, knowing she had lost. He didn't even speak her name.

"Take this traitor away," he said.

Chapter 15

MARK

Mark Novak chewed his lip, pacing the room. This wasn't going according to plan. In fact, this was the worst possible outcome. Ivanov had always been unpredictable. Worse, he had the ear of Head Servant Lunde. He looked at his guest. The young man sat in his lounge chair and seemed to be making an effort to remain calm.

"What do you want me to do?" Mark asked. Evan Hordvik stared back at him.

"What do you think? Counselor, you know she's no traitor. But she must have seen something she wasn't supposed to. You know what they do to people if they have, especially if they aren't Moon blood."

Mark nodded, though he had no illusions that Moon people would be exempt if someone like Ivanov found out they were a threat. So the question remained, should he write her off, or take a risk trying to save her?

"But what do you want *me* to do?" he repeated.

"I want you to go right now and stop this. Go to the First Janissary, or above him if necessary. If anyone can do it, sir, it's you," Hordvik said. Mark continued pacing. He knew the young man was right. Susan Atlas was too special to let go so easily.

"If you need a character witness, I'll be more than willing," Hordvik said. That made Mark chuckle.

"No, thank you, Head Tacticus. That would only put you on the spot with her. I do appreciate your concern, but please don't do anything reckless."

Mark stopped pacing. He suddenly knew what to do. It was a risky option, and it depended on finding out if blood really was thicker than water, something Mark wasn't entirely certain of. Also, there were a lot of unknowns and even more guesswork. He couldn't see any other options, though. He smiled at Hordvik.

"First of all, relax. She's a known heroine, remember? The ceremony was broadcast all over the Covenant. They need to take that into consideration," Mark said. The young man shook his head.

"That won't save her," he said. Mark nodded.

"You're right, it won't save her. But it will buy her some time."

Mark saw the confusion in the younger man's face. In fact, it was Mark and young Hordvik who needed time. Time to put Mark's plan into effect.

"Your father has access to security level four, right?" he asked. Hordvik nodded. Of course. The Hordviks were a prominent family in the Covenant, had been since long before the Descent, and Evan's father sat on the Luna Council, an advisory board that some thought had far too much influence over the head servant. Mark, though not a formal member of the Council due to his lack of Moon heritage, had often consulted with them, but as time went by, he tended to work more directly with the head servant, especially since Alexej Lunde trusted his advice and the two had developed a good working relationship.

"It is time for you and your father to reconcile your differences," he said. Hordvik just stared at him.

"I don't care what you have to do. But after all, you already took the first step coming here to Legacy. Now, all you have to do is reach out personally."

"Why?" Hordvik asked. Mark furrowed his brows.

"Your father has a level-four security access. I do, as well, but I am monitored. Your father is in charge of all top-level security monitoring. I'm sure, if you showed an interest in intel and security work, you could manage to persuade him to let you into level three."

"I could get level three easily without asking him for it," Hordvik replied. "I already need that clearance in my current work, so I was planning on getting it from the personnel security office."

Mark sat down next to him shaking his head.

"Even better, but don't go to PS. Instead, go to your

father and make up. Then, once you have gone through the motions, done all the crying and embracing and all that, you mention your work. He has level four; there is nothing you need to hide from him. Work, got it?" he said. Hordvik just stared in front of him, and Mark knew this had to be difficult. Father and son hadn't spoken for many years, and now, he expected the young man to try and heal such a wound in what must seem like an instant.

"From there, you have to feel your way forward. When the timing is right, you complain that personnel security has given you an inadequate clearance. No bitching, just hint at not being able to do you job properly." Hordvik turned toward Mark. It looked like he was beginning to grasp what he had in mind.

"So, instead of PS granting me level-three access, I circumvent them by going through my father. That way, I would get clearance immediately, and they wouldn't even know I had it until he remembered to inform them." Mark grinned, nodding eagerly.

"And even if he did it at once, with all the forms and the bureaucracy, it would easily take two to three days until monitoring took effect." Mark leaned back. The young man was a good ally—intelligent, well trained—and he had very good connections. This could actually work.

"In that time, you can move undetected all over the

level-three system, as long as you cloak your movements. And you will have time to hide your tracks afterward," he said.

"Don't you think my father would be monitoring me personally? You know how he can be," Hordvik said.

"Sure, that can happen. But in that case, you will have to make up a story and stick with it. Curiosity, perhaps, or a more desperate need to know. But whatever you do, don't let him see your connection to me, or to Miss Atlas. Remember, he wants to believe you're back on track. And he might even help you hide some of your moves, as long as he believes your story."

"So what is it you want me to do once I have access?" Hordvik asked. Mark walked over to his desk, and scribbled a note. He handed it over to the young man, who looked at it.

"An English name," he said. Mark nodded.

"Level three includes certain drone footage from Warden territory. In at least one of those files, this person should be part of that footage. I want you to get me the location of that particular file and the key code for it." He smiled. "You find that file, and I will take care of Miss Atlas."

SUE

"Get on your feet," the guard said as the door burst open. Sue jumped. She had been so lost in thought, she hadn't noticed the buzz of the locks or the ping of the key.

"You're lucky, Tacticus. Someone up high decided to give you a second chance. Probably since you're a decorated hero. So let's move it, shall we?"

Sue got up. She didn't have any of her things here, and come to think of it, she didn't own anything important, anyway. She exited her cell and saw there were two more guards outside. She let them lead on, and they all walked down the hall and into an elevator. Once the doors slid shut, one of the guards touched a panel, and the elevator began moving. Up, she noted.

Ping.

The doors opened, and she felt the breeze blow in, straight through her clothes. It was a cold day, and she wasn't dressed for it. The chill felt good, though, after three days in a cell with no windows and no communication except for a few short phrases with the guards. First Janissary Ivanov hadn't even come to gloat, which surprised her. She squinted in the harsh light and looked out at the skyline of Legacy, the capital city of the Covenant. The view, even from inside the elevator, was magnificent. The Moon people had built an empire out of the ashes, and if she hadn't known of the cost, she would have been impressed. Now though, all she felt was disgust.

She took a few steps out of the elevator and saw the tethered airship off to the right. And a man in long robes standing beside the boarding cage. A man she had seen a few times before. The man who had sent orders for her to come to Legacy. She walked over to him, the guards two steps behind. Counselor Novak motioned for the guards to stand back, and they left her alone with him.

"Counselor," she said, dipping her head slightly.

"Atlas," he replied, his face grave.

"Some predicament you got yourself into," he said. She didn't know what to say, so she kept quiet.

"Luckily, I managed to persuade the head servant that neither imprisonment nor execution of a decorated heroine, whose reputation is known throughout the Covenant, would serve to please the public. So we found another solution." A half-smile appeared on his face.

"Suffice to say, First Janissary Ivanov wasn't pleased," he said, and winked. She stared at him, forgetting the chill for a moment.

"Why did you do this for me?" Sue asked.

"Well, that's a long story. But let me just say this: I think you have it in you to bring about change. A change for the better." And she realized he must know.

"But what can I do? I'm not even a citizen? And if I ever get there, I will still be English," she said. She met his eyes, old and wise, despite the ageless face.

"And the Moon blood rules, right?" he said quietly.

She nodded. He turned and looked at the skyline, and she came and stood beside him, covering herself with her arms to keep the cold out. Novak spoke again, while staring out at the sprawling city.

"Sometimes, one has to take great risks in order to produce great change. By taking you out from under the murderous clutches of Ivanov, I took a great risk. Someday there will be payback. And a common friend of ours—you don't need to know the name—has taken great risks as well in the past few days." He turned to face her. "Now it's your turn." He turned and nodded to the airship.

"Once you get on that ship, your life is in dire peril," he said. She looked at him, trying to read that look in his eyes. Concern? Determination? He was a hard man to read.

"If they were smart, they would shoot the airship down today. But they won't because they think they have another way. A way that will look better in the eyes of the public. But it can happen at any time. So be ready."

For what, she was about to say, but an airman came out of the cage, and motioned for her to enter.

Counselor Novak leaned over and whispered in her ear before she stepped away.

"Remember, Susan. Bliss is ignorance. Not the other way around."

Chapter 16

SUE

For the last hour, Sue had been blindfolded, and she squinted against the harsh sunlight when it was removed. The air felt warmer than back in Legacy, and for a moment, she feared that she had been sent back to Charlestown, kicked out of Service. Or worse, that she had been sent further south, to the Corpus, to slave under the whip until she wasted away.

Then she saw the uniforms. Not spit shine, disciplined like the Janissaries, but rather a loose resemblance binding individualistic bents together. She looked around. Some of the men wore beards, and many were laughing or chatting loudly. A large, bearded man in a colorful shirt stood waiting, but she noticed that even he wore elements of uniform than identified him as part of this outfit.

The Wardens.

"Welcome, Initiate Atlas," the man said.

"Sorry about the rank, but our way is different. You'll have to work your way up." He grinned, a perfect set of teeth showing through his beard. And now that she looked closer, she saw that he was Moon blood, although the ruffled facade hid it well.

"Having read your résumé, I have no doubt you will excel here, as well. In fact, we have already decided on your specialization." She looked at him quizzically.

"Why, you are a natural born ranger, of course. But let's get you set up first." He led her on, and they walked through the camp. The man talked and Sue listened. She was too stunned, realizing what lengths Counselor Novak must have gone to in order to get her transferred here instead of to the Corpus, or simply disappear.

"You will have a few days to learn the ropes. Then, the rangers will come pick you up. You will only become a full Warden once you have field experience. Unfortunately, Warden experience is the only thing that counts. We're quite busy these days, though, so it shouldn't take long."

They reached a large building, red brick walls and few windows.

"All right then, here we are. A senior Warden will help you get settled in, and then you will spend the next few days with the other initiates. Just follow their lead, but don't let these slackers drag you down with them." He laughed.

"You see, most initiates from the last batch have already progressed to full Warden. Those who remain just didn't make the cut yet. Oh, we will make Wardens of them still. Sometimes, it just takes a little more time," he said. Sue smiled and was about to open the door when the man, who still hadn't introduced himself, stopped her.

"And by the way, Atlas. I understand you have a friend here, Warden Wagner, right?" She nodded.

"He's in the middle of his specialization and made full Warden just a few weeks ago. He is very busy, so please, just leave him be for now."

Then he turned and walked away, without waiting for a reply. Sue watched him for a moment, wondering what his role could be, and decided he looked like someone she ought to listen to. His natural authority needed no rank, and the way he acted left no doubt that this guy held a very high rank—he just didn't have a need to flash it around.

She entered the building, wondering what life here would be like. She wished she could start anew, but she remembered Counselor Mark Novak's warning. She knew she had stepped too far, and it was only a matter of time before they made a move on her.

Inside, she was greeted by a senior Warden who took her to her room, empty for now. She sat down on the bed and sighed. There was no such thing as starting anew. Every human being was a product of their experiences, and hers had already paved a path from which there would be no return.

DAVE

He was scanning through the system, in search of something he knew should be there, somewhere. The file containing the drone footage would be located on level three or four, he was certain of it. But where?

Thankfully, his search shouldn't raise suspicions. He was Tech after all, and searching for weaknesses in the system was one of his tasks. It was all part of his training. If he found the file, though, that was something else. Given that he managed to break the security on the file itself, what would they do if they discovered he's seen the contents?

But he needed to know. A man had been killed, and Dave needed to find the murderer. Someone had done this, and that someone should be punished for the crime. It was a convenient way of doing it, shooting someone in the back, while most were occupied with the monsters.

Kirilov was a prime suspect, of course. But it could just as easily have been one of the other seniors. He never learned their names, but he figured if he found the file, it would be marked with a date and time. That should be enough to open up an investigation. Even if all the suspects were Moon blood, he didn't think such evidence could be disregarded.

He sighed. There was always the possibility that the

file had been deleted, in which case recovering it would be even more difficult. But not impossible. There was no way to completely erase every trace of data. There would always be bits and pieces that led to new bits and pieces. In time, he figured most of the file could be restored, even if the perpetrator had deleted it. He was better at this than any of them.

No way anyone should get away with it.

He stretched his back and looked at the clock on the wall behind him. Hasle had left two hours ago, to get some new wiring he needed. He'd probably gone to lunch while he was out. Dave's stomach growled, telling him he should go as well.

He got up and stretched some more. Sitting in front of the screen, immersing himself in strings of data, sometimes made him lose track of time. He needed a break.

He walked outside. The sun was shining, and he considered going to sit for a while in the sun, a quick nap would feel wonderful right now. But his stomach growled again. He smiled. *All right*, he thought, *lunch then*.

There were several places to grab lunch, and while most chose the cafeteria in the center of camp, he preferred to grab something from the shop nearby and take his lunch outside. He walked over, and five minutes later, he stood by the counter to check out his pack of food. The old man behind the counter, probably a Warden veteran who had chosen to stay after Service, smiled at him, and he put his finger on the scanner. An upside down image appeared, and the man glanced quickly at it. Dave smiled at it all, knowing that he shopped here at least three or four times a week. He didn't think the ID verification was really necessary. Not around here.

"Two and a half credits," the man said. Dave nodded and tapped the green YES icon right below the image of his fingerprint. The old man nodded, and Dave walked out with his pack. He looked around, wondering if he should try a new spot today. For variation.

Then he saw her.

She looked different, walked differently, and she had this air of experience around her that told him she had been through things. Seen things. Done things.

But it was her all the same.

"Sue!" he shouted. She turned.

"Dave!" she said. She looked around, hesitating, before she walked over.

"I'm not supposed to disturb you..." she said.

"Disturb? Sue, what are you doing here?"

"Long story. You look good, Dave," she said, smiling. He felt his cheeks flush.

"Sue, I never really got to thank you, back then," he

said. She had saved him, at Initiation Day, when he was about to be sent off to the Corpus. That was a debt he would never be able to pay back.

"Don't worry about it," she said. "Maybe you can look out for me this time, since you're a full Warden and all."

"What, they made you an initiate?" he said, surprised. She nodded.

"Yeah. I'll head out with the rangers in a few days, though. Soon as I get some field experience here, they will raise me to full Warden." Dave cocked his head.

"Yes, that sounds like a good idea. I don't know what you did in the Janissaries, but I guess you'd be a natural ranger. So a few days, eh?"

"They will come pick me up. I have no idea where the rangers are."

"Me, either. I have a friend with the rangers, Liz. Maybe you'll run into her."

"I might," Sue said, looking around again.

"I'm sorry Dave, but I should get going. I hope to see you again before I go," she said. Dave smiled.

"Well, let's make sure of it. How about you come here for lunch tomorrow?" he said.

"Sorry, I have a class then. What about the day after?" she asked.

"It's a date," he replied, before he flushed again.

"Oh, I didn't mean, like a date…" Sue laughed.

"Of course. Let's just meet, okay? Day after tomorrow, lunch, right here," she said. Dave smiled again.

"Okay."

Sue walked off, and Dave stood for a moment, wondering what could have brought her here. But he was happy to see a friend from back home and looked forward to talking more with her. Day after tomorrow.

He walked toward his regular spot and sat down with his lunch. Soon his mind was elsewhere, coming up with ideas for how to find hidden files in a system set up with traps and some of the most advanced security the Covenant could muster. He had a few options, but it was like searching for the proverbial needle in a haystack. He sighed. It could take months, or even years. But he was not going to give up.

~

It was the day after he had met Sue, and it was getting late. Dave was thinking of her as he moved among the files, cloaking his movements from anyone tracking him, while rummaging around for traces that would lead to the files he was searching for. He had donned the VR headset, which made it easier to see unlikely traces, which deleted and moved files often left behind. Especially when the programmer was an amateur or in a hurry. Dave suspected the killer would be both.

He was following a particularly interesting trail when a purple sphere appeared in his peripheral vision. It looked insubstantial, but there was something inside it. He couldn't tell what it was, though.

The sphere moved closer, and Dave cursed silently. He must have set off some kind of trap, drawing security protocols toward his location. He waited, hoping it would pass him by, that it was just some random algorithm or a disconnected program of sorts. When it kept moving straight toward him, he began to remove the VR headset.

"Please don't," a booming voice said. He stopped.

"Wagner, is it?" the sphere said, its voice softer now.

"Who is this?" Dave asked, curious and concerned at the same time. He had the perfect explanation for being here, with his Tech training and all, but he also knew the killer might be around. Or someone who'd react to his searching through files he wasn't supposed to know of, instead of performing tasks set by Hasle, his superior.

"Wait just a second... There," the voice said. *What was that about?* Dave thought. Then he noticed the transparent, almost invisible shimmer surrounding both him and the sphere.

"What the hell did you just do? Who are you? What do you want?" Dave rattled off the questions, angry now. Mostly because he didn't understand how it was done. He looked at the sphere, and a figure slowly appeared inside it. A man. A face. A familiar face. A face he'd seen so many times, but always on screen, never for real.

"Counselor," he said, still not moving. Too perplexed to move.

Counselor Mark Novak smiled briefly, but he didn't waste time.

"So, have you found what you are looking for?" he asked. Dave shook his head, taken aback and unable to come up with a rational explanation. He realized Counselor Novak *knew* something.

"Perhaps I can help?" Novak continued, then shook his head.

"Horrible thing, what happened. Do you have a suspect?" he asked. Dave's jaw dropped.

"How do you know?"

The counselor just smiled.

"All right... I believe it must have been Kirilov, or one of the other seniors..." he said, and Novak cut him off.

"Moon people. So, you are accusing Moon people of murder. That's a serious accusation, Wagner." The counselor let it hang in the air. This was too much. If Novak knew this much, he must know...

"Sir, how come you know so much? How do you know they were all Moon people? Kirilov, sure, the name gives him up. I never gave you the names of the others, though," he said, a chill running down his spine.

Novak still smiled.

"Yes, how did I know..." Novak became completely solid, as if he was really there.

"A few days ago, something happened. You see, a common friend of ours has learned something not many people know. And I have really high hopes for this person, so much that I had to look for ways to save her, but gently, so as not to put myself in harm's way."

Sue, Dave thought. Who else?

"So I had someone look for a file with you in it, since I knew you were her friend. I knew you would be willing to help her, especially when I found out about how she helped you once. And since I know more about the Wardens, more about the Covenant in fact, than most people alive, I knew where to find you. And I knew what else I would find..."

Dave waited for Novak to finish up and saw his face change from a smile into something else.

Outrage, Dave realized.

"For too many years, unimaginable crimes have been committed. I mean to see the end of it, and once you see what I have to show you, you will help me. And you will help Miss Atlas, lest she ends up like Greer."

It was like a blow to the head. Someone wanted Sue

dead—but why? And could he trust this man? He mustered up the courage to ask one question.

"Who would want to kill Sue?" he asked. The counselor grimaced.

"Who did she insult when she saved you from being sent to the Corpus?" *Of course*, Dave thought. The First Janissary seemed the type to bear a grudge. Sue must have given him an excuse, and he had seized the opportunity. He dared another question.

"How do you know about Greer? Have you seen the drone footage?" Novak shook his head.

"No, I haven't seen it. Greer's name is in the report. I saw that," he said. Dave felt a pang of irritation.

What does he really know? Dave wondered. *Is he playing me?*

"Sir, I'm getting confused. What is happening here? Please don't play games with me," he said. He didn't care if he insulted the man. He needed answers. He needed the truth.

Mark Novak nodded, as if he understood Dave's confusion. He sighed.

"Susan Atlas has become a problem in Legacy. She has discovered things… Things that are considered a serious threat to the security and integrity of the Covenant. So now, they want her dead. And not just Ivanov," he said. Dave nodding gravely, waiting for him to continue.

"But she has become a symbol, a hero, in the eyes of the public. So they can't just execute her. They need her to maintain the image of heroism, while at the same time, they need to get rid of her. Before she becomes too dangerous. So I nudged them along, helped them come to the only possible solution, one that would actually benefit them more than if she had just been a good Janissary. A good martyr." He chuckled, without mirth.

"A transfer. The hero from the northern border goes south to perform heroic deeds on the western border, as well, keeping the Covenant safe, guarding the Rift," he said.

"So you sent her here?" Dave asked. Novak smiled.

"Yes, in a way. By order of Head Servant Lunde himself, fulfilling the wishes of a young patriotic soldier, and sending her to the next frontline." The old man shook his head slightly, and closed his eyes.

"Where she is to be killed on her first mission," Dave said, now clearly seeing the logic. "The heroine dies in combat, while protecting the Covenant against its enemies. It is the perfect way." Novak produced a small sphere. Inside, letters and numbers danced.

"This is the key code and the location of the video file you've been looking for. The one that reveals the truth. When you are finished with it, you will know what to do to save her.

And yourself," Novak said. Dave touched the sphere, instantly copying its contents to his secure folder, hidden behind another file. It would be safe, at least until someone did a thorough search.

"And you're still saying you haven't seen it?" Dave said.

"I haven't. But I know what's there. I've seen dozens like it. Just remember, once you use the key, it might trigger an alert. So don't do it until you're absolutely certain you are ready. And be prepared to face the consequences."

Chapter 17

DAVE

Dave removed the VR headset, and put it gently beside his monitor. He still didn't entirely trust Counselor Novak, but how could he not do this? How could he not look at the video? Especially since hearing what they were planning for Sue. He quickly locked the system and got up. Then he walked over to the fridge and grabbed a water bottle. He almost emptied the bottle, his thoughts racing, going through every detail of his virtual encounter with the Legacy Counselor. However weird it all seemed, it made sense. He'd never even heard of anyone transferring to the Wardens. If you messed up in any of the Services, it was off to the Corpus or out of the Services altogether.

He checked to see if Hasle was there. Only when Dave was absolutely sure he was all alone, did he unlock the system again. He checked his messages for the tenth time in the last fifteen minutes. He went through a couple of short documents, but his mind was elsewhere, and it was time to end the procrastination.

He opened his private folder and went through the first levels of security. Then he inverted a subfolder, decrypting the access path to another folder, and finally, invisible beside the latter, he tapped his screen lightly.

A key prompt jumped up. He quickly entered the key, and finally, the folder he had received from Novak appeared. He opened it. Two files. One video file and a simple text file. He opened the text file and memorized the twelve-digit code. Then he closed the text file, and let his finger hover over the video file icon for a second.

Don't do it until you're absolutely certain you are ready, Novak had said. Dave tapped the icon, and another key prompt jumped up. Twelve digits. He began entering numbers, letters, signs.

Be prepared to face the consequences. Yeah, right.

How could he be ready? There was no such thing.

Are you certain you wish to continue? Bold letters in front of his eyes. A blinking question mark. Red no, green yes.

He tapped the green icon.

For a moment, the screen was black. Then the video began. The chirping of a bird was the first thing he heard, before the image adjusted and he could see.

He was looking at himself, from the back. Then he was looking at the others. He recognized some of them. Kirilov, Scott, Greer.

Guns aimed, fingers on the triggers.

The sound suddenly stopped on the video. Dave

looked at the volume indicator on the left. He swiped it up to max. Still nothing. Must be a technical error. Perhaps a separate file that hadn't synced when he opened the video. He moved the cursor back, just a couple of seconds of playing time and pressed play again, hoping this would work.

As the sound returned, the view changed. Something moved on the far side of the clearing.

A man appeared, ragged clothes hanging loose from his shoulders. Zoom in. Shaggy beard, hollow cheeks. Dave could instantly tell this man was starving. He was looking at the man entering the clearing again. Zoom in. The man's eyes, scanning the area in front of him. Then he signaled something, and the others followed him out of the brush, into the clearing. Men, women, children. A baby in the arms of its mother.

Warily, one step at a time, everyone looking around, even the smallest children. All except for the baby, sleeping soundly.

What were they so afraid of?

He turned the sound down, just enough to hear. He knew what was coming next.

The view zoomed out again as the first shots rang out. The man was the first to fall.

Dave didn't blink.

Somehow, in the back of his mind, he had realized as

soon as he'd seen the poor man.

"What the hell is this?" he heard Greer scream through the commotion. The camera switched to Greer, who stood up, his night vision goggles pushed up on the top of his helmet. Dave mouthed Greer's next words silently.

"What have you done to us? Why…" The drone was filming from behind, and the explosion from Greer's chest only showed the red haze outside of his silhouette, for which Dave was thankful. Then he saw—all too clearly—Kirilov's face as he looked around, making sure his rifle quickly pointed away from the dead man.

Dave realized he was clenching the edge of his desk so hard that his knuckles had turned white. He felt the bile in his throat rising and swallowed hard. *What have you done to us?* he thought, a single tear running down his cheek. He gritted his teeth and made himself watch as all the Wardens kept firing at those poor people. Had he stopped firing once he heard Greer's screams? He didn't remember. He didn't think so. And what did it matter?

He began to look away as the slaughter went on, but decided against it. He needed to see this. It was the truth. The raw, unfiltered truth.

He remembered the words now. From when they got the so-called vaccine. Juri, the medical assistant, who had to be subdued and dragged off by three Wardens.

Ignorance is Bliss.

And then, after the carnage, just as he passed out. A soft voice in his ear.

Ignorance is Bliss.

It had some truth to it. But it wasn't *the* truth. It was all a lie. A big, horrible lie.

So this was how they "protected" the Covenant. This was how they kept out those from the outside. Why? What was the point of this?

He watched through it all, forcing himself to see every single piece of footage, even the parts that made him shake and sob. Eyes open, gritting his teeth, breathing slowly to keep the contents of his stomach down, not giving himself a moment's respite.

The video ended abruptly, as the airship returned to pick them up.

Silence. The icon completely still on the monitor.

As if nothing had happened.

He had been searching for a murderer, and what he had found was more than he could have imagined.

Kirilov was Greer's murderer.

Then it struck him, like a blow to the head. They were all murderers. All except Greer, who hadn't fired a single shot. Greer, who had cried out. Who had seen everything for what it was.

Dave didn't open the file again, but he began mentally replaying the scenes, and everything that had happened up to that horrible scene.

After seeing the truth, the pieces began to fall into place.

Greer had thrown off his night vision goggles. Dave remembered that annoying flicker in his own goggles. A glitch on the edge of the screen. The screen that made humans look like monsters.

The syringe before leaving camp. A serum to get the mind ready for what was coming, to tear down the defenses of logic. Then the blue pill, another dose of medication, numbing the mind just enough to accept what you saw. Enough to not question it, but not enough to limit combat efficiency. And finally, something he only remembered now that everything began to return to him, the red pill, which blurred the memory, made it difficult to remember the details.

You have to see for yourself, everyone had said.

Dave had seen it all. And now he remembered.

The words of Counselor Novak came back to him. *Once you use the key, it might trigger an alert.*

Dave looked around and shook his head. Of course, somewhere an alert would go off, but not anything audible. No sirens or alarms wailing. Just a silent notification of what had happened.

Someone could be bursting in that door any moment.

Be prepared to face the consequences.

Dave quickly copied the file onto a memory card and stuck it inside his boot. Then he locked the computer and got up.

Time to face the consequences.

~

Dave made sure nobody was following before he stalked out. He didn't know which building Sue was in, but there was really only one place she could be. He walked quickly around his building and kept walking, passing the shop on his way toward the buildings surrounding the square. There, he had to make a guess. There were three buildings, occupied by younger Wardens, mostly those specializing for security. Then there was one section in the building to his left, in which initiates were staying. That would be where all those who hadn't made specialization yet would be. He didn't have anything to go by, so he just guessed she would be among the other initiates. He strode toward the entrance. Except for one guard busily reading a book, there was no form of security in place. There was no need for it inside the fences, since the Warden camp was heavily protected outside the camp proper.

He entered and quickly scanned the boarding list just

inside the door.

Susan Atlas, init.W, 2nd floor, room 206.

He took off his boots and climbed the stairs in his socks, taking two steps at a time, moving quietly while keenly aware that anyone meeting him would wonder when they saw him carrying his boots. He didn't have time to take every precaution, though, and the way he figured, the best he could do to remain unnoticed was to be quick. He half-sprinted through the hallway, finding the door to room 206. He carefully opened it. No squeak. Seems they took better care of this building than the one he'd been assigned to when he was an initiate.

He stepped inside. It was dark, so he couldn't see who was in the beds.

"Sue," he whispered, too loud. He winced at his own stupidity. There was no answer, though. Someone coughed, and he froze, holding his breath. He could be detected any moment, but he had to take a chance. He tiptoed along the beds, as quietly as he could manage. He almost stumbled on a pair of shoes as he leaned over each bed, one by one, to see in which one she lay.

He found her on the far side of the room and lightly touched her shoulder. She stirred for half a second before her eyes shot open. A frown displaying her puzzlement made him hold a finger in front of his mouth, quietly urging her not to speak. She nodded once.

"Come with me," he whispered in her ear. No need to add quickly or quietly. She would understand something was up.

Sue got out of bed and grabbed her pants and a T-shirt before they quietly made their way out. Sue closed the door carefully and put on her clothes. Then they moved back through the hallway and down the stairs, past the guard. Dave led the way, and soon, they were outside, sneaking through shadows toward the southern part of camp, where there was a small grove where they might finally be able to talk.

"All right," Sue whispered once they were far enough away from anyone who could overhear.

"What's going on? Why did you drag me out of bed like this?"

Dave bit his lip, wondering where to start. He'd only had a vague notion of how to go about this, and now he felt stuck. He looked at her, wondering what she had done to make Legacy want her dead.

"Why did they send you here?" he asked instead. She squinted and smiled, a mirthless smile.

"Of course. I should have guessed you wouldn't buy into it all." Then she sat down, motioning for him to sit beside her.

"Can I trust you, Dave?" she asked. He nodded. Of

course she could trust him. She seemed to know it, too, even though she'd asked. Sue took a deep breath.

"I discovered it's all a lie," she said. He remained quiet to let her speak, and she continued.

"The Covenant. All of it. The Moon people. They enslaved us, and we think they saved us." She shook her head.

"Yeah, that's one way of putting it..." Dave said. He didn't know how to tell her all the horrible details about his own experience, so he asked more about hers instead.

"So, any idea when the rangers will come pick you up?" he asked. Sue cocked her head.

"In fact, I do. One of them, Harald something, told me to get a good night's sleep, because we're moving out tomorrow morning." She yawned. "Which is just... in a couple hours. Dave, I really need to get going. We can't change the Covenant, you know. We just have to come to terms with how it is. But I really need some sleep before I go."

Dave cut her off.

"If you go with them, you won't be coming back," he said. She hesitated for a moment.

"What are you talking about?" she asked.

"I think you discovered something, and someone up in Legacy thinks you might be dangerous to the Covenant or something." He paused for a moment. "They want you dead, Sue. They just brought you here because they need to make it look like you die in combat. They want to make a martyr out of you." She cocked her head, and Dave couldn't tell whether she believed him or not. He pressed on.

"But it's not combat," he said. He swallowed, trying to hold back the flood.

"It's a slaughter. Innocent people…" he said, voice quivering.

"They made us shoot… made us believe that they were…" He couldn't find the words and felt the memories jumble about, making him unsure of what was what.

"They drug us, make us believe we are fighting monsters. But there are no monsters, just innocent people. People from the West, from beyond the Rift. And afterward, they gave us some kind of pill that made us forget."

"Ignorance is bliss," Sue whispered, watching him as if she seemed to remember something herself. Dave nodded.

"Yeah, that's what they say. But it's the other way around," he whispered back.

"Bliss must be the drug, the one that changes our memories and our perception, making us their tools."

They sat quietly for a moment before Sue spoke.

"But what can we do? I mean, it's been like this for decades, centuries probably. In a few hours, it's my turn. I may be killed or I may not, and there's not a thing we can do about it."

"We could run away," he said. Sue just smiled, a sad smile.

"And go where?"

Dave shook his head.

"I don't know. Anywhere but here." He hesitated. He had told her so much already, but she didn't seem ready to do anything about it. Then again, she hadn't seen the video.

"I have spoken to someone who's trying to save you," he said, waiting for her reaction. There was none.

"You will die tomorrow, Sue. I've seen it happen. I know how they do it, and if you go back, you will not live to see the end of tomorrow." Sue exhaled deeply.

"This is just... How do you know?" she asked.

"A man from Legacy told me. A very old man," he answered. They looked at each other in silence for a moment. She knew who he was talking about, Dave realized.

"So I have to run then," she said slowly, as if trying out the idea in her mind. "But you should stay, Dave. You shouldn't risk your life for me."

He shook his head.

"Too late," he said.

"I've seen the truth. So I have to die, as well."

Chapter 18

SUE

They lay covered in shadows, hidden from moonlight and floodlights, watching how the guards moved. Time was running out. If they didn't get out of camp soon, daylight would ruin whatever slight chance they had. And once someone discovered they were missing, alarms would go off everywhere.

Sue knew their chances were slim. They were deep inside Warden territory, and running on foot would be all but impossible. With sensors and trackers everywhere, airships, rangers, Bliss, tampered goggles that would make anyone a stone-cold killer, they would have no chance. They had to not only get out of camp, but as far away from the Warden camp as possible.

They only had one chance, and a slim one at that.

That was the reason they were watching the guards assigned to airpad security.

In a few minutes, the airship would arrive. And if Dave's assessments were correct, the rangers would set off an alarm, like they did when Dave went through his field experience. They would have a small window of opportunity, while the alarm wailed and the initiates were gathered. Once the rangers didn't find her, they would know something was up, and all hell would break loose. She figured they would have a couple of minutes to do it, at best.

"The rangers will come looking," Dave said. She kept counting the steps the guards used between the fixed points on their rounds and wasn't paying attention to his words. Although the Wardens didn't seem as keen on routines as the Janissaries, all guards tended to have routines to some extent. Sue thought she might have figured these out, but it was just a hunch. Once it happened, they would have to go through with it, no matter how the guards acted.

She heard a deep buzzing, like a high-voltage current, and then the airship appeared.

"Get ready," she said. She wished they had a weapon, any weapon.

The airship slowed until it hovered just above the airpad. A serviceman tethered the anchor, and the cage lowered. Three Wardens, rangers, heavily armed and wearing combat gear and helmets, stepped out and walked toward the square. As soon as they rounded the corner, Sue tensed.

"Okay, Dave. Remember, run like hell and don't let anything stop you. Count your steps. Once you reach twenty, dive and stay down, like we agreed. The crates will cover us. Keep counting. Once you reach twenty again, you get up and run until you reach the cage. Press the UP button. If one of us doesn't make it, the other must keep going. We only have one chance. Those topside won't know we're coming; they'll expect it to be one of the rangers or something." Dave nodded intently, and she realized she had never seen him looking so... competent. He'd always been smart, but right now, he looked like he knew his stuff, even with this wild plan of theirs.

It was a long shot, and they both knew it. But if they were to have any chance whatsoever, this plan had so succeed. They knew the alternative was worse, and this way, at least they would be doing *something*.

She gritted her teeth and flexed her muscles. Now or never, do or die.

They leapt simultaneously, just as the last guard rounded a corner, moving out of sight.

She ran as quickly as her legs could carry her, counting silently, not even looking over to see if Dave was holding up. Her eyes were fixed on the crates, stacked high just on the edge of the airpad. Halfway there already. She chanced a glance to her right and noticed Dave was right next to her. She hadn't expected him to be so physically fit, but then again, he'd been through basic training, as well. And he'd made full Warden, and not just because he was clever.

Twenty.

She threw herself against the crates and immediately

began to try controlling her breath, slowing it while taking deep lungfuls. Dave bumped into her as he landed, but neither of them spoke a single word. Sue didn't even dare take a peek to see if the guards had moved as anticipated. She kept counting. Ten, eleven, twelve…

Dave got something that looked like a knife from his pocket and gripped it hard. A thin screwdriver. Not much of a weapon, but better than nothing. Their eyes met, and she nodded. It seemed Dave was as determined as she. Considering what he had told her, she wasn't surprised.

Eighteen. She took a deep breath. Nineteen. She flexed again, ready for the final sprint. *Their final desperate move*, she thought.

Twenty.

They both got up. Dave was a half second quicker, and pushed her down again, hard.

One of the guards was still there.

Dave held up five fingers in front of her face. Four. Three. Two.

"Now," he mouthed silently.

One.

They got up again.

The coast was clear.

And then they ran, sprinting even harder than before. Sue wondered if they would have anything left once they reached the cage. It didn't matter. Unless they reached it undetected, they didn't stand a chance.

Dave stumbled and fell.

Oh no, she thought, hesitating.

They had agreed that if one of them didn't make it, the other would keep going.

She realized she couldn't do it.

Sue grabbed his arm and pulled him up on his feet. He took a step and winced.

The guards would be back any second.

She took his screwdriver in one hand and held him across the waist with the other. She dragged him along as quickly as she could. His face contorted in pain, but he managed to keep quiet.

Just a few more steps to go.

They reached the cage.

Sue grabbed the handle and opened the hatch.

The guard standing just inside the door looked at them, surprise apparent and confusion slowing him down.

His rifle moved, slightly.

Sue stabbed him in the throat, while knocking his hand away.

He lost his grip on the weapon, and Dave grabbed it before it could fall.

Sue held a hand over the guard's mouth as he slid

down to the floor, then she pulled the screwdriver out, letting the blood run freely.

The guard went silent, and Sue pushed the UP button. The cage rocked slightly as it ascended, and Sue looked at Dave. He looked like he was in a lot of pain, but he checked the gun and got a better hold on it, while supporting his weight against the side of the cage. She was probably a better shot, but he looked like he knew what he was doing.

The cage shook again as the ascent ended. The hatch opened, and they both got out as quickly as they could. There was no one there.

"The pilot," Dave whispered. He winced again as he tried to move away from the cage. He shook his head and handed her the gun.

Sue grabbed the gun, recognizing it as one of the weapons the QRF at Camp Gustavson had used. She knew it well enough. She walked as silently as she could toward the front, where the pilot would be.

The pilot compartment's hatch crashed open as a short man, about thirty, red headed and puffy faced, leapt out, holding a small sidearm.

"Hold it right there," he shouted. Sue kept her own gun aimed at him.

"Take it easy," she said, a sinister grin creeping forth, "and consider this. If we surrender, we're dead. If you put your gun down, you might live. So who do you think is more desperate?" Her words came out calmer, colder than she felt.

The pilot seemed to consider his options for a moment, and then he slowly spread his arms, changing his grip on the gun. Holding it with two fingers, he carefully laid it on the deck.

"We don't have all night," Sue said impatiently, motioning him to return to the pilot's compartment. She followed him inside, still pointing her gun at him.

"First of all, kill the comms and all tracking and positioning," she said. The pilot hesitated, but then he pushed a few buttons.

"All right, that's good. So. I want you to enable cloaking. No lights, of course. Just cut the tethers and move out."

A muffled bang from outside as the tethers were cut by the emergency charges.

The airship engines were silent, even as they began moving.

"Where do you want me to go?" he asked. Sue considered for a moment. They hadn't discussed that, only that they needed to get away.

"Just move out. Doesn't matter where to," she said. The pilot hunched and pushed the control buttons, making the airship speed up. They saw the camp below as the ship turned. It still looked quiet down there, even though alarms were probably going off right now. Soon everyone in the Covenant would be searching for them.

Where was the one place they would never think to look?

"Take us south," she said quietly.

~

Sue and Dave sat inside the pilot compartment, right behind the pilot, who was struggling to keep a straight course without the use of many of his usual instruments. They were both exhausted, and neither of them had spoken much since their escape. The sun was rising in the east, its first rays shining through the port windows, giving the entire compartment a glow, as if it were on fire. Sue imagined she could see the Rift far to the west, but she couldn't be sure. And there was no way she wanted to go anywhere near it, since the terrain on the eastern side would be teeming with Wardens. She looked at the pilot again. He hadn't spoken since she had given him the order to head south. It seemed he had resigned himself to do what he was told.

Sue felt hollow, and she had no idea what to do next, only that they needed to go as far south as the airship would take them. She ached to go home, to see her mother and Jason, but she knew that wasn't going to happen. She would only endanger them, as well. There were no good options anymore, only better or worse bad ones.

It was Dave who finally broke the silence.

"They erased our memories," he said. She turned toward him.

"They made us do all these things, and then they made us forget." Sue thought about her own experience. She had somehow remembered, once she saw the image of Renee, but until then, it had all been hazy, like a bad dream you couldn't quite recall.

"They enslaved us, and then they made us believe they saved us," she said, remembering Renee's words. Dave nodded.

"Yeah, that's probably the worst part. They reinvented history completely." He seemed to consider his words.

"But don't you think that's what anyone would do? I mean, if the English had come from somewhere safe, and saved the Moon people. Don't you think we would have told our story, made us into saviors? That's just a small step from making us rulers and them our subjects…" He trailed off.

"I'd like to think we would be different," Sue said. "You know, make different choices."

"I don't know," Dave said and looked out the window.

"Sometimes, it's all about perspective. Other times,

it's all about seeing the truth. You cannot un-see the truth," he said.

"Unless they give you Bliss," Sue replied dryly. "Ignorance is Bliss, remember?"

Dave half-smiled.

"Someone told me it's the other way around," he said.

The pilot turned, a concerned look on his face.

"I hate to interrupt, but we're crossing into Corpus territory," he said.

"Seems you guys know about Bliss. Maybe you should consider whether that would be better than this? There are ways to make you forget permanently, you know. You just repeat the sequence until you're blank, and you can start all over again." Sue looked at him quizzically.

"I didn't know pilots learned about Bliss," she said, "even if you are Moon blood."

He grimaced.

"We all learn about Bliss. Without it, the Covenant would unravel," he said.

Sue had a hard time holding back her temper, but Dave shot her a hard look. She remained silent, letting Dave speak instead.

"So... what if it did?" Dave asked. The pilot looked stunned by the response.

"Why, that would be a disaster. Not just for us, but

for you, as well. What do you think would happen if there were no Janissaries to protect us from the savages to the north? Or if the Wardens didn't keep the westerners out? What if the Corpus didn't produce all those things we need? And what about population control? There's a reason no non-citizens can live past fifty. We wouldn't be able to feed them all." He stopped when neither of them spoke and turned back to his instruments, shaking his head.

Sue was too tired to argue.

There was a world of difference between them, and no argument would settle that. Nobody knew what the future held, but when even the past was a lie, what about the present?

All she knew was that their entire world had proved to be a lie. Sue and Dave had somehow seen through it, and they couldn't take it anymore.

The lies that killed so many and enslaved the rest were too much to bear.

For they had seen the truth, and there was no going back after that.

Epilogue

MARK

Mark Novak sat in the soft leatherback chair, facing his old friend and partner, keeping his thoughts to himself, studying the head servant's face as the latter studied the report on his infopad. It had been personally delivered by the master warden himself; a sign of how seriously they took this. Mark kept a straight face. He had come to like Head Servant Lunde as a person, even though he didn't see how the man opposite from him could be capable of reforming the Covenant. Like himself, the head servant was too entrenched in the old guard. Even more so, come to think of it. Those of the Moon people who had been through the Youth Rebellion tended to think of themselves as the progressive force. Those who had changed the original Lunar society. Those who had led their people back. Those who had taken charge.

They were rulers now, bent on protecting their vision of Utopia. And Mark wondered how long they had left.

"You should get the treatment, Mark. I can see it's about time," his friend said, brow furrowed.

Mark waved him off.

"I can't. Not now. There's too much going on," he said. Mark knew it was time, but he just couldn't see himself taking months off to stay in a hospital, frozen for weeks at a time. He had to stay on top of this. If he went into treatment now, it could all be over before he got out. And if that happened, everything would be wasted. The world would go up in flames, just because he feared the effects of old age. He knew what would come, but not when or in what order. The first signs would be shocking to anyone of the Moon people, and even some who had earned their citizenship. The wrinkles, the loss of energy. He almost smiled, but managed to keep a straight face. It was absurd to him, but then again, he had lived at a time when all that was normal.

That would just be the beginning, though. Once his organs began to fail, or perhaps dementia came for him… Now, that would be serious. But he would have to face it for as long as he had to, and hope he still had time once the storm passed.

Head Lunde just shook his head, but didn't reply. Mark watched him get up, walk over to his desk, and have a quick glance at his infopad, before he returned to his own chair.

"Nothing?" Mark asked.

"Nothing. It's like they vanished into thin air. Up in smoke. Poof," Lunde said, gesticulating with his hands, like a magician from the Legacy Circus. Mark looked away, losing himself in the crackling fire from that old fireplace, like he often did when the two of them sat there. That was one good thing he could say about his friendship with Alexej Lunde; the two of them were able to sit in the same room and think. Not chatter away all the time—just think. It was a rare thing, to have a friend he could sit with and not talk all the time. Had he ever had a friend like that?

Perhaps.

He thought of an old friend. Even though he'd been the most careful, sharp, cunning man he'd ever known, he had lost everything, even his life, in the end. Would Alexej end up the same way? Would Mark?

He was afraid the answer had to be yes, even if nobody could tell how long it would take.

But sooner or later, all men's sins catch up with them.

And their sins were aplenty.

"I still think you should take it. The treatment. I think I can handle this, Mark," the head servant said, a concerned look on his face.

Mark shook his head again.

"Alexej… Nobody knows more about this than I, and I'm telling you, I will be fine. Just a while longer. There's too much happening right now. And you do need me," he said.

"I wondered what happened to them. Where did they go?" Lunde said absently.

Mark stared at the fireplace again.

"I don't know," he said. "But I know one thing. There's a storm coming."

~

Join me on christensenwriting.com!

Be the first to know about new releases, and download your FREE e-book!

When the world ends, what do you do when you realize you are still alive?

In a world devastated by natural disaster, only the most stubborn refuse to give up. When Ed Walker learns that others have been preparing for the disaster for years, he begins to realize finding them may be his only shot at survival. But time is running out...

In a dying world one man makes a choice to keep going, hoping against all odds there might be a future after all.

Alive is a novella loosely based on events in Exodus by Andreas Christensen, but can also be read as a standalone.

Download your FREE copy from http://christensenwriting.com

Before you leave, I would like to ask you a favor.

In the new world of publishing, word of mouth may be the most important factor in a story finding its readers. If you enjoyed these stories, please consider leaving a review. It doesn't matter if it's short. The fact that someone read it, and liked it, could mean the difference between another reader deciding to try it, or moving on to the next story. And it would be much appreciated.

About the Author

Andreas Christensen is a Norwegian science fiction author. He is the author of the Exodus Trilogy, in which a divided Earth must face the ultimate extinction event. Then, on distant Aurora, more than 40 light years away, humanity must come to terms with its legacy of violence and division and begin to build a new world.

The RIFT Saga takes place more than two centuries after the events in Exodus, and the keen reader will already have noticed the connections...

You can find his complete and up to date bibliography on christensenwriting.com.

You can find Andreas Christensen here:

Website:

http://www.christensenwriting.com

Blog:

http://www.christensenwriting.com/blog

Amazon:

http://www.amazon.com/author/andreaschristensen

Twitter:

http://www.twitter.com/achr75

Facebook:

http://www.facebook.com/christensenwriting